RAZORBILL

An Imprint of Penguin Random House

RAZORBILL

An Imprint of Penguin Random House
Penguin.com

ISBN: 978-1-59514-551-2

Printed in the United States of America

1 3 5 7 9 10 8 6 4 2

Also by Jay Asher

Thirteen Reasons Why
The Future of Us (with Carolyn Mackler)

TO:

JoanMarie Asher, Isaiah Asher,
and Christa Desir,
the three gift-bearers of
this Christmas story

Dennis and Joni Hopper,
and their sons, Russel and Ryan,
for the inspiration

FROM:

a grateful boy

CHAPTER ONE

"I hate this time of year," Rachel says. "I'm sorry, Sierra. I'm sure I say that a lot, but it's true."

Morning mist blurs the entrance of our school at the far end of the lawn. We stay on the cement pathway to avoid damp spots in the grass, but Rachel's not complaining about the weather.

"Please don't do this," I say. "You'll make me cry again. I just want to get through this week without—"

"But it's not a week!" she says. "It's two days. Two days until Thanksgiving break, and then you leave for a whole month again. More than a month!"

I hug Rachel's arm as we continue walking. Even though I'm the one leaving for another holiday season far from home, Rachel pretends like it's *her* world that gets turned upside-down each year. Her pouty face and slumped shoulders are entirely for my benefit, to let me know I'll be missed, and every year I'm grateful for her melodrama. Even though I love where I'm going, it's still hard to say goodbye. Knowing my best friends are counting the days until I return does make it easier.

I point to the tear in the corner of my eye. "Do you see what you did? They're starting."

This morning, when Mom drove us away from our Christmas tree farm, the sky was mostly clear. The workers were in the fields, their distant chainsaws buzzing like mosquitoes, cutting down this year's crop of trees.

The fog came in as we drove lower. It stretched across the small farms, over the interstate, and into town, carrying within it the traditional scent of the season. This time of year our entire little Oregon town smells like fresh-cut Christmas trees. At other times, it might smell like sweet corn or sugar beets.

Rachel holds open one of the glass double doors and then follows me to my locker. There, she jiggles her glittery red watch in front of me. "We've got fifteen minutes," she says. "I'm cranky and I'm cold. Let's grab some coffee before the first bell."

The school's theater director, Miss Livingston, not-so-subtly encourages her students to drink as much caffeine as needed to get their shows together on time. Backstage, a pot of coffee is always on. As the lead set designer, Rachel gets unrestricted access to the auditorium.

Over the weekend, the theater department finished their

performances of *Little Shop of Horrors*. The set won't be broken down until after Thanksgiving break, so it's still up when Rachel and I turn on the lights at the back of the theater. Sitting on the stage, between the flower shop counter and the big, green, man-eating plant, is Elizabeth. She sits up straight and waves when she sees us.

Rachel walks ahead of me down the aisle. "This year, we wanted to give you something to take with you to California."

I follow her past the empty rows of red cushioned seats. They obviously don't care if I'm a blubbering mess during my last few days of school. I climb the steps to the stage. Elizabeth pushes herself up, runs over, and hugs me.

"I was right," she tells Rachel over my shoulder. "I told you she'd cry."

"I hate you both," I tell them.

Elizabeth hands me two presents wrapped in shiny silver Christmas paper, but I already kind of know what they're giving me. Last week, we were all in a gift shop downtown and I saw them looking at picture frames the same size as these boxes. I sit down to open them and lean against the counter under the old-fashioned metal cash register.

Rachel sits cross-legged in front of me, our knees almost touching.

"You're breaking the rules," I say. I slide a finger beneath a fold in the wrapping of the first gift. "We're not supposed to do this until after I get back."

"We wanted you to have something that will make you think of us every day," Elizabeth says.

"We're kind of embarrassed we didn't do this when you first started leaving," Rachel adds.

"What, back when we were babies?"

During my very first Christmas, Mom stayed home with me on the farm while Dad operated our family Christmas tree lot down in California. The next year, Mom thought we should stay home one more season, but Dad didn't want to be without us again. He would rather skip the lot for a year, he said, and rely solely on shipping the trees to vendors across the country. Mom felt bad, though, for the families who made a holiday tradition out of coming to us to buy their trees. And while it was a business, Dad being the second generation to run it, it was also a cherished tradition for both of them. They met, in fact, because Mom and her parents were annual customers. So every year now, that's where I spend my days from Thanksgiving to Christmas.

Rachel reclines, setting her hands on the stage to prop herself up. "Are your parents still deciding about this being the last Christmas in California?"

I scratch at a piece of tape that holds down another fold. "Did the store wrap this?"

Rachel whispers to Elizabeth loud enough for me to hear, "She's changing the subject."

"I'm sorry," I say, "I just hate thinking about this being our last year. As much as I love you, I would miss going down there. Besides, all I know is what I've overheard—they still haven't mentioned it to me—but they seem pretty stressed about finances. Until they make up their minds, I don't want to get my heart set either way."

If we hang on to the lot for three more seasons, our family will have run that spot for thirty years. When my grandparents first bought the lot, the little town was in a growth spurt. Cities much closer to our farm in Oregon already had established lots, if not an abundance of them. Now everything from supermarkets to hardware stores sells trees, or people sell them for fund-raisers. Tree lots like ours aren't as common anymore. If we let it go, we'd be doing all of our business selling to those supermarkets and fund-raisers, or supplying other lots with our trees.

Elizabeth puts a hand on my knee. "Part of me wants you to go back next year because I know you love it, but if you do stay we'd all get to spend Christmas together for the first time."

I can't help smiling at the thought. I love these girls, but Heather is also one of my best friends, and I only see her one month out of the year when I'm in California. "We've been going down there forever," I say. "I can't imagine what it would be like to suddenly . . . not."

"I can tell you what it would be like," Rachel says. "It'll be senior year. Skiing. Hot tubbing. In the snow!"

But I love our snowless California town, right on the coast, just three hours south of San Francisco. I also love selling trees, seeing the same families come to us year after year. It wouldn't feel right to spend so long growing the trees only to ship them all off for other people to sell.

"Sounds fun, right?" Rachel asks. She leans close to me and wiggles her eyebrows. "Now, imagine it with boys."

I snort-laugh and then cover my mouth.

"Or not," Elizabeth says, pulling back Rachel's shoulder. "It could be nice to have it just us, a time without any boys."

"That's pretty much me every Christmas," I say. "Remember, last year I got dumped the night before we drove to California."

"That was horrible," Elizabeth says, though she does laugh a little. "Then he brings that homeschool girl with the big boobs to winter formal and—"

Rachel presses a finger to Elizabeth's lips. "I think she remembers."

I look down at my first present, still mostly wrapped. "Not that I blame him. Who wants to be in a long-distance relationship over the holidays? I wouldn't."

"Although," Rachel says, "you did say there are some good-looking guys who work on the tree lot."

"Right." I shake my head. "Like Dad will let that happen."

"Okay, no more talking about this," Elizabeth says. "Open your gifts."

I pull up a piece of tape, but my mind is now on California. Heather and I have been friends literally since we can remember. My grandparents on Mom's side used to live next door to her family. When my grandparents passed away, her family took me in for a couple of hours each day to give my parents a break. In exchange, their house got a beautiful Christmas tree, a few wreaths, and two or three workers to hang lights on their roof.

Elizabeth sighs. "Your presents. Please?"

I tear open one side of the wrapping.

They're right, of course. I would love to spend at least one winter here before we all graduate and move off to wherever. I've had dreams of being with them for the ice-sculpting contest and all the other things they tell me about that go on around here.

But my holidays in California are the only time I get to see my *other* best friend. I stopped referring to Heather simply as my winter friend years ago. She's one of my best friends, period. I used to also see her a few weeks every summer when visiting my grandparents, but those visits stopped when they passed away. I worry I may not be able to enjoy this season with her, knowing it might be my last.

Rachel stands up and walks away across the stage. "I need to get some coffee."

Elizabeth yells after her, "She's opening our presents!"

"She's opening *your* present," Rachel says. "Mine has the red ribbon."

The first frame I open, with the green ribbon, contains a selfie of Elizabeth. Her tongue sticks out sideways while her eyes look in the opposite direction. It's like almost every other photo she takes of herself, which is why I love it.

I press the frame against my chest. "Thank you."

Elizabeth blushes. "You're welcome."

"I'm opening yours now!" I shout across the stage.

Walking slowly toward us, Rachel carries three paper cups of steaming coffee. We each take one. I set mine to the side as Rachel sits back down in front of me, and then I begin to open her present. Even though it's only one month, I am going to miss her so much.

In Rachel's photo, her beautiful face is sideways, partially blocked by her hand as if she didn't want the picture taken.

"It's supposed to look like I'm being stalked by the paparazzi," she says. "Like I'm a big-time actress coming out of a fancy restaurant. In real life, though, there would probably be a huge bodyguard behind me, but—"

"But you're not an actress," Elizabeth says. "You want to do set design."

"That's part of the plan," Rachel says. "Do you know how many actresses there are in the world? Millions. And all of them are trying so hard to get noticed, which is a total turnoff. One day, while I'm designing sets for some famous producer, he'll take one look at me and just know it's a waste to keep me behind the camera. I should be in front of it. And he'll take full credit for discovering me, but I actually *made* him discover me."

"What concerns me," I say, "is that I know you believe it's going to happen just like that."

Rachel takes a sip from her coffee. "Because it is."

The first bell rings. I gather the silver wrapping paper and crumple it into a ball. Rachel carries that and our empty coffee cups to a trash can backstage. Elizabeth puts my frames into a paper grocery bag and then rolls down the top before handing it back to me.

"I assume we can't stop by before you leave?" Elizabeth asks.

"Probably not," I say. I follow them down the steps, and we take our time walking up the aisle to the back of the theater. "I'll be in bed early tonight so I can work a couple of hours before school tomorrow. And then we leave first thing Wednesday morning."

"What time?" Rachel asks. "Maybe we—"

"Three a.m.," I say, laughing. From our farm in Oregon to our lot in California, it's about a seventeen-hour drive, depending on bathroom breaks and holiday traffic. "Of course, if you want to get up that early . . ."

"That's okay," Elizabeth says. "We'll send you good thoughts in our dreams."

"Do you have all your assignments?" Rachel asks.

"I believe so." Two winters ago, there were maybe a dozen of us migrating tree-lot kids at school. This year, we're down to three. Thankfully, with so many farms in the area, teachers are used to accommodating different harvest times. "Monsieur Cappeau is worried about my ability to *pratique mon français* while I'm gone, so he's making me call in once a week for a chat."

Rachel winks at me. "Is that the only reason he wants you to call?"

"Don't be gross," I say.

"Remember," Elizabeth says, "Sierra doesn't like older men."

I'm laughing now. "You're talking about Paul, right? We only went out once, but then he got caught with an open can of beer in his friend's car."

"In his defense, he wasn't driving," Rachel points out. Before I can respond, she holds up her hand. "But I get it. You saw that as a sign of impending alcoholism. Or bad decision making. Or . . . something."

Elizabeth shakes her head. "You are way too fussy, Sierra."

Rachel and Elizabeth always give me a hard time about my standards with guys. I've just watched too many girls end up with guys who bring them down. Maybe not at first, but eventually. Why waste years or months, or even days, on someone like that?

Before we reach the double doors that lead back into the halls, Elizabeth takes a step ahead and spins toward us. "I'm going to be late for English, but let's meet up for lunch, okay?"

I smile because we always meet up for lunch.

We push our way into the halls and Elizabeth disappears into the bustle of students.

"Two more lunches," Rachel says. She pretends to wipe tears from the corners of her eyes as we walk. "That's all we get. It almost makes me want to—"

"Stop!" I say. "Don't say it."

"Oh, don't worry about me." Rachel waves her hand

dismissively. "I've got plenty to keep me busy while you party it up in California. Let's see, next Monday we'll start tearing down the set. That should take a week or so. Then I'll help the dance committee finish designing the winter formal. It's not theater, but I like to use my talents where they're needed."

"Do they have a theme for this year yet?" I ask.

"Snow Globe of Love," she says. "It sounds cheesy, I know, but I've got some great ideas. I want to decorate the whole gym to look like you're dancing in the middle of a snow globe. So I'll be plenty busy until you get back."

"See? You'll hardly miss me," I say.

"That's right," Rachel says. She nudges me as we continue to walk. "But you'd better miss me."

And I will. For my entire life, missing my friends has been a Christmas tradition.

CHAPTER TWO

The sun barely peeks up from behind the hills when I park Dad's truck on the side of the muddy access road. I set the emergency brake and look out on one of my favorite views. The Christmas trees begin a few feet from the driver's side window and continue for over a hundred acres of rolling hills. On the other side of the truck, our field continues just as far. Where our land ends on either side, more farms carry on with more Christmas trees.

When I turn off the heater and step outside, I know the cold air is going to bite. I pull my hair into a tight ponytail, tuck it down the back of my bulky winter jacket, bring the hood over my head, and then pull the drawstrings tight.

The smell of tree resin is thick in the wet air, and the damp soil tugs at my heavy boots. Branches scratch at my sleeves as I pull my phone from my pocket. I tap Uncle Bruce's number and then hold the phone against my ear with my shoulder while I pull on work gloves.

He laughs when he answers. "It sure didn't take you long to get up there, Sierra!"

"I wasn't driving that fast," I say. In truth, taking those turns and sliding through mud is way too fun to resist.

"Not to worry, honey. I've torn up that hill plenty of times in my truck."

"I've seen you, which is how I knew it would be fun," I say. "Anyway, I'm almost at the first bundle."

"Be there in a minute," he says. Before he hangs up, I can hear the helicopter motor start to turn.

From my jacket pocket, I remove an orange mesh safety vest and slip my arms through the holes. The Velcro strip running down the chest holds it in place so Uncle Bruce will be able to spot me from the air.

From maybe two hundred yards ahead, I can hear chainsaws buzz as workers carve through the stumps of this year's trees. Two months ago, we began tagging the ones we wanted cut down. On a branch near the top we tied a colored plastic ribbon. Red, yellow, or blue, depending on the height, to help us sort them later while loading the trucks. Any trees that remain untagged will be left to continue growing.

In the distance, I can see the red helicopter flying this way. Mom and Dad helped Uncle Bruce buy it in exchange for his help airlifting our trees during the harvest. The helicopter keeps us from wasting land with crisscrossing access roads, and the trees get shipped fresher. The rest of the year, he uses it to fly tourists along the rocky coastline. Sometimes he even gets to play hero and find a lost hiker.

After the workers ahead of me cut four or five trees, they lay them side-by-side atop two long cables, like placing them across railroad tracks. They pile more trees on top until they've gathered about a dozen. Then they lace the cables over the bundle and cinch them together before moving on.

That's where I come in.

Last year was the first year Dad let me do this. I knew he wanted to tell me the work was too dangerous for a fifteen-year-old girl, but he wouldn't dare say that out loud. A few of the guys he hires to cut the trees are classmates of mine, and he lets them wield chainsaws.

The helicopter blades grow louder—*thwump-thwump-thwump-thwump*—slicing through the air. The beat of my heart matches their rhythm as I get ready to attach my first bundle of the season.

I stand beside the first batch, flexing my gloved fingers. The early sunlight flashes across the window of the helicopter. A long line of cable trails behind it, dragging a heavy red hook through the sky.

The helicopter slows as it approaches, and I dig my boots into the soil. Hovering above me, the blades boom. *Thwump-thwump-thwump-thwump.* The helicopter slowly lowers until the metal hook touches the needles of the bundled trees. I raise my arm over my head and make a circular motion to ask for more slack. When it lowers a few more inches, I grab the hook, slip it beneath the cables, and then take two large steps back.

Looking up, I can see Uncle Bruce smile down at me. I point at him, he gives me a thumbs-up, and then up he goes. The heavy bundle pulls together as it lifts from the ground, and then it sails away.

A crescent moon hangs over our farmhouse. Looking out from my upstairs window, I can see the hills roll off into deep shadows. As a child, I would stand here and pretend to be a ship's captain watching the ocean at night, the swells often darker than the starry sky above.

This view remains constant each year because of how we rotate the harvest. For each tree cut, we leave five in the ground and plant a new seedling in its place. In six years, all of these individual trees will have been shipped around the country to stand in homes as the centerpiece of the holidays.

Because of this, my season has different traditions. The day before Thanksgiving, Mom and I will drive south and reunite with Dad. Then we'll eat Thanksgiving dinner with Heather and her family. The next day we'll start selling trees from morning to night, and we won't stop until Christmas Eve. That night, exhausted, we'll exchange one gift each. There isn't room for many more gifts than that in our silver Airstream trailer—our home-away-from-home.

Our farmhouse was built in the 1930s. The old wooden floors and stairs make it impossible to get out of bed in the middle of the night without making noise, but I stick close to the least creaky side of the stairs. I'm three steps from the kitchen floor when Mom calls to me from the living room.

"Sierra, you need to get at least a few hours of sleep."

Whenever Dad's not here, Mom falls asleep on the couch with the TV on. The romantic side of me wants to believe their bedroom feels too lonely when he's gone. My nonromantic side thinks falling asleep on the couch makes her feel rebellious.

I hold my robe around me and slip my feet into tattered sneakers by the couch. Mom yawns and reaches for the remote control on the floor. She turns off the TV, which blackens the room.

She clicks on a side lamp. "Where are you going?"

"To the greenhouse," I say. "I want to bring the tree in here so we don't forget it."

Rather than loading our car the night before we leave, we place all of our bags near the front door so we can look them over one more time before the drive. Once we hit the highway, the road ahead is too long to turn back.

"And then you need to go right to bed," Mom says. She shares my curse of not being able to sleep if I'm worried about something. "Otherwise, I can't let you drive tomorrow."

I promise her and close the front door, pulling my robe tighter to keep out the cold night air. The greenhouse will be warm, but I'll be inside only long enough to grab the little tree, which I recently transplanted into a black plastic bucket. I'll put that tree by our luggage and then Heather and I will plant it after dinner on Thanksgiving. This will make six trees, which started on our farm, that now grow atop Cardinals Peak in California. The plan for next year has always been to cut down the first one we planted and give it to Heather's family.

That's one more reason this can't be our last season.

CHAPTER THREE

From outside, the trailer may look like a silver thermos tipped on its side, but the inside has always felt cozy to me. A small dining table is attached to the wall at one end, with the edge of my bed doubling as one of the benches. The kitchen is compact with a sink, refrigerator, stove, and microwave. The bathroom feels smaller every year even though my parents upgraded for a bigger shower. With a standard shower, it would have been impossible to reach down and wash my legs without doing stretches first. At the other end of the trailer from my bed is the door to Mom and Dad's room, which has barely enough space for their bed, a small closet, and a footstool. Their door is shut now, but I can hear Mom snoring as she recovers from our long drive.

The foot of my bed touches the kitchen cabinet, and there's a wooden cupboard above it. I press a large white thumbtack into the cupboard. On the table beside me are the picture frames from Rachel and Elizabeth. I've connected them with shiny green ribbon so they'll hang one on top of the other. I tie a loop at the end of the ribbon and hook it onto the thumbtack so my friends back home can be with me every day.

"Welcome to California," I tell them.

I scoot to the head of my bed and slide the curtains apart.

A Christmas tree topples against the window and I scream. The needles scratch the glass as someone struggles to pull the tree upright again.

Andrew peeks around the branches, probably to make sure he didn't bust the glass. He blushes when he sees me, and I glance down to make sure I put on a shirt after showering. Over the years I have taken a few morning showers and then walked around the trailer in a towel before remembering a lot of high school guys work right outside.

Last year, Andrew became the first and the last guy to ask me out down here. He did it with a note taped to the other side of my window. It was meant to look cute, I guess, but what I pictured was him tiptoeing in the dark mere inches from where I slept. Thankfully, I was able to tell him it wouldn't be smart to date anyone who works here. That's not an actual rule, but my parents have mentioned a few times how uncomfortable that might be for everyone involved since they work here, too.

Mom and Dad met when they were my age, and he worked with his parents on this very lot. Her family lived a few blocks away, and one winter they fell so hard for each other, he returned for baseball camp that summer. After they married and took over the lot, for extra help they began hiring ballplayers from the local high school who wanted extra holiday cash. This was never a problem when I was young, but once I entered puberty, new and thicker curtains were hung up around the trailer.

While I can't hear Andrew, I see him mouth "Sorry" from the other side of the window. He finally gets the tree upright and then shimmies the stand back a few feet so the lower branches don't touch any tree around it.

There's no reason to let our past awkwardness keep us from being cordial, so I slide the window partly open. "So you're back for another year," I say.

Andrew takes a look around, but there's no one else I could be talking to. He faces me, putting his hands in his pockets. "It's nice to see you again," he says.

It's great when workers return for subsequent seasons, but I am careful not to give this one the wrong idea again. "I heard some other guys from the team came back, too."

Andrew looks at the nearest tree and plucks a couple of needles. "Yep," he says. He petulantly flicks the needles to the dirt and walks away.

Rather than let this get to me, I slide the window open further and close my eyes. The air out there will never smell exactly like home, but it does try. The view is very different, though. Instead of Christmas trees growing on rolling hills, they're propped up in metal stands on a dirt lot. Instead of hundreds of acres of farmland stretching to the horizon, we have one acre that stops at Oak Boulevard. On the other side of the street, an empty parking lot stretches toward a grocery store. Since it's Thanksgiving, McGregor's Market closed early today.

McGregor's has been in that spot since well before my family began selling trees here. It's now the only non-chain market in town. Last year, the owner told my parents they might not be in business when we returned. When Dad called home a couple of weeks ago to say he made it, the first thing I asked was whether McGregor's was still there. As a child I loved when Mom or Dad took a break from selling trees and walked me across the street for groceries. Years later, they would hand me a shopping list and I would go over on my own. The last few years it's been my responsibility to make that list as well as shop.

I watch a white car drive across the asphalt, probably to make sure the market really is closed for the evening. The driver slows as he passes the storefront, then speeds back across the lot to the street.

From somewhere within our trees, Dad shouts, "Must've forgot the cranberry sauce!"

Throughout the lot, I can hear the baseball players laugh.

Every year on this day, Dad jokes about the frustrated drivers speeding away from McGregor's. "But it won't be Thanksgiving without pumpkin pie!" Or, "I guess someone forgot the stuffing!" The guys always laugh along.

I watch two of them carry a large tree past the trailer.

21

One has his arms buried in the middle branches while the other follows, holding the trunk. They both stop walking so that the one in the branches can adjust his grip. The other guy, waiting, looks to the trailer and catches my eye. He smiles and then whispers something to the first guy that I can't hear but that causes his teammate to also look my way.

I desperately want to make sure my hair isn't a tangled mess even though I have no reason to impress them (no matter how cute they are). So I politely wave and then walk away.

On the other side of the trailer door, someone scrapes the bottoms of their shoes on the metal steps. Although it hasn't rained since Dad set things up this year, the ground outside always has damp spots. A few times each day, the tree stands get filled with water and the needles are sprayed with misters.

"Knock-knock!"

I barely get the door unlatched before Heather yanks it open and squeals. Her dark curls bounce as she raises her arms and then hugs me. I laugh at her high-pitched excitement and follow her as she kneels at my bed for a closer look at the photos of Rachel and Elizabeth.

"They gave me those before I left," I tell her.

Heather touches the top frame. "This is Rachel, right? Is she supposed to be hiding from the paparazzi?"

"Oh, she would be so happy to know you figured that out," I say.

Heather scoots to the window so she can see outside. She taps on the glass with her fingertip and one of the ballplayers looks our way. He's carrying a cardboard box marked "mistletoe" to the green-and-white tent we call the Bigtop. That's where we ring up customers, sell other merchandise, and display the trees flocked with artificial snow.

Without looking at me, Heather asks, "Did you notice how hot this year's team is?"

Of course I noticed, but it would be so much easier if I hadn't. If Dad even thought I was flirting with one of the workers, he would make the guy thoroughly clean both outhouses in hopes that the stink would keep me away—which it would.

Not that I would want to date someone down here, whether he worked for us or not. Why put my heart into something fate will only tear apart Christmas morning?

CHAPTER FOUR

After we stuff ourselves with Thanksgiving dinner, and Heather's dad makes his annual "hibernate through the winter" joke, all of us move to what have become our traditional destinations. The dads clear and wash the dishes, partly so they can continue nibbling at the turkey. The moms head to the garage to start bringing in far too many boxes of Christmas decorations. Heather runs upstairs to grab two flashlights, and I wait for her at the bottom of the stairs.

From the closet near the front door, I take down a forest green hoodie Mom wore on our walk over. Yellow block letters spell LUMBERJACKS, her college mascot, across the chest. I pull the sweatshirt over my head and hear the back door in the kitchen open, which means the moms are returning. I quickly look upstairs to see if Heather's on her way down.

We were trying to leave before they returned and asked for help.

"Sierra?" Mom calls.

I tug my hair up through the collar. "About to leave!" I shout back.

Mom carries in a large transparent plastic tub full of newspaper-wrapped decorations.

"Is it okay if I borrow your sweatshirt?" I ask. "When you and Dad go back, you can wear mine."

"No, yours is so thin," she says.

"I know, but you won't be out nearly as long as us," I say. "Plus, it's not even that cold."

"*Plus*," Mom says sarcastically, "you should have thought of that before we came over."

I begin to take off her sweatshirt, but she motions for me to keep it on.

"Next year, stay and help us with . . ." Her words trail off.

I shift my eyes to the stairs. She doesn't know I've heard the conversations between her and Dad, or between both of them and Uncle Bruce, about whether or not we'll open the lot next year. Apparently it would have made the most sense to pull up stakes two years ago, but everyone's hoping things will bounce back.

Mom sets the plastic tub on the living room carpet and pops off the top.

"Sure," I say. "Next year."

Heather skips down the stairs in the faded red sweatshirt

she only wears this one night a year. The cuffs are in tatters and the neckline is stretched. We got it at a thrift shop soon after my grandpa's funeral, when Heather's mom took us shopping to cheer me up. Seeing her in it always feels bittersweet. It reminds me of how much I miss my grandparents when I'm down here but also how great a friend Heather has been to me.

She stops at the bottom of the stairs and offers me a choice of two small flashlights, purple or blue. I take the purple one and put it in my pocket.

Mom unrolls a newspaper-wrapped snowman candle. Unless Heather's mom changed decorating plans for the first time in forever, that candle will go in the front bathroom. The wick is black from the one brief moment Heather's dad lit it last year. At the first smell of burning wax, her mom pounded on the bathroom door until he blew it out. "It's a decoration!" she shouted. "You don't light decorations!"

Mom looks at the kitchen and then to us. "If you want to make it out of here, you'd better go now," she says. "Your mom's looking for her entry in this year's ugly Christmas sweater contest. Apparently she's got a winner."

"How bad is it?" I ask.

Heather scrunches her nose. "If she doesn't win, those judges have no sense of horrendous."

When we hear the back door open, we scramble out the front door and slam it shut behind us.

Next to the welcome mat is the small tree I carried over

from the lot. Earlier, I transferred the tree out of the plastic bucket, so its roots are now bound in a scratchy burlap sack.

"I'll carry it up the first half," Heather says. She picks up the basketball-sized bag and settles it in the crook of her arm. "You can carry that little shovel thingie you brought."

I pick up the gardening trowel and we head out.

🌲

Less than halfway up Cardinals Peak, Heather says it's time to switch. I slide my flashlight into my back pocket and then we shift the tree into my arms.

"You got it?" she asks. When I nod, she takes the trowel from my hand.

I adjust my hold and we continue our hike up the hill, which the locals adorably call a mountain. We keep to the center of the packed-dirt access road, which will loop around three times before we reach our spot. The moon looks like a clipped fingernail tonight, barely lighting this side of the hill. When we circle to the other side, we'll need our flashlights even more. Now, we mostly use them to scare away anything small that we hear scurrying in the bushes.

"Okay, so the guys you work with are forbidden," Heather says, as if continuing a discussion that's already been playing in her head. "So help me brainstorm other people you can . . . you know . . . spend time with."

I laugh and then carefully pull the flashlight from my back pocket and aim it at her face. "Oh. You were serious."

"Yes!"

"No," I say. I check her face again. "No! For one, we're busy all month; there's no time. For another—and most important—I live in a trailer on a tree lot! No matter what I say or do, my dad is right there."

"It's still worth trying," she says.

I tilt the tree to keep the needles out of my face. "Plus, how would you feel if you knew you had to dump Devon right after Christmas? You'd feel horrible."

Heather pulls the small trowel from her back pocket and taps it against her leg as we walk. "Since you brought it up, that's kind of the plan."

"What?"

She lifts a shoulder. "Look, you've got your high standards about how relationships should be, so I'm sure I sound all—"

"Why does everyone think my standards are high? What does that even mean?"

"Don't get all prickly." Heather laughs. "Your standards are one of the reasons I love you. You've got this solid . . . I don't know . . . moral foundation, and that's great. But it makes someone planning to dump her boyfriend after the holidays feel kind of bad. You know, in comparison."

"Who plans a breakup an entire month ahead of time?" I ask.

"Well, it'd be cruel to do it right before Thanksgiving," she says. "What would he say at dinner with his family, 'I feel thankful for having my heart broken'?"

We walk several steps in silence as I think about this. "I

guess there's never a good time, but you're right that there are worse times. So how long have you been thinking about it?"

"Since right before Halloween," she says. "But we had such great costumes!"

The moonlight fades as we round the hill, so we shine the lights closer to our feet.

"It's not that he's a jerk or anything," Heather says. "Otherwise I wouldn't care about sticking around for the holidays. He's smart—even if he doesn't act like it—and gentle and cute. It's just that he can be so . . . boring. Or maybe it's more like clueless? I don't know!"

I would never judge anyone else's reasons for a breakup. Everyone wants or needs different things. The first person I broke up with, Mason, was smart and funny, but also a bit needy. I thought I wanted to feel needed, but that gets exhausting real fast. I learned that it's much better to feel wanted.

"How is he boring?" I ask.

"Let me put it this way," she says. "If I were to describe his boringness to you, the words coming out of my mouth would be more exciting."

"Really?" I say. "Then I cannot wait to meet him."

"And that's why you need a boyfriend while you're here," she says. "So we can double-date. Then my dates won't be so dull."

I consider how awkward it would be to start seeing someone here, knowing there's an expiration date attached. If I wanted that, I could have said yes to Andrew last year.

"I'm going to pass on the double-dating," I say. "But thanks."

"Don't thank me yet," she says. "I'll probably bring it up again."

After the next turn, which takes us near the top of Cardinals Peak, Heather and I step off the narrowing dirt road and into knee-high brush. She sweeps her flashlight back and forth. What sounds like a small rabbit bounds away.

Another dozen steps and the brush mostly clears. It's too dark to see all five Christmas trees at once, but when Heather's flashlight hits the first one, my heart warms. She slowly scans the beam until I see them all. We spaced them several feet apart so one won't overshadow another in the sunlight. The tallest is already a few inches taller than me, and the smallest barely reaches my waist.

"Hey, guys," I say as I walk among them. Still holding the newest tree with one arm, I touch the needles of the other trees with my free hand.

"I came up last weekend," Heather says. "I pulled some weeds and loosened the ground a bit so tonight will be easier."

I set the burlap sack on the dirt and then face Heather. "You are becoming Little Miss Farmer Girl."

"Hardly," she says. "But last year it took us forever to clear the weeds after dark, so—"

"Either way, I'm going to pretend you enjoyed yourself," I say. "And whatever the reason, you would not have done it unless you were an awesome friend. So thank you."

Heather politely nods and then hands me the trowel.

I look around until I find the perfect spot. A new tree, I believe, should always get the best view of what's happening below. After I kneel into the dirt, which is soft thanks to Heather, I begin digging a hole large enough to contain the roots.

The last two years we made the trek, we took turns carrying the tree. Before that we wheeled it up here in Heather's red wagon. It has become like my own little tree farm, a way to keep a part of me here after my family heads back north.

I wonder again if, next year, I'll have the chance to cut down the oldest tree.

This season was supposed to be perfect, not bogged down with what-ifs. They're all around me, though, in everything I do. I don't know how to fully enjoy any of these moments without wondering if it's the last.

I untie the twine that holds the burlap around the roots. When I peel the fabric away, the roots stay mostly in place, still covered in soil from back home.

"I'm going to miss these hikes," Heather says.

I set the tree into the hole and spread out some of the roots with my fingers.

Heather kneels beside me and helps me scoop dirt back into the hole. "At least we have one more year," she says.

Unable to look at her, I sprinkle another handful of soil around the base of the tree. I clap the dirt from my hands and then sit on the ground. Pulling my knees to my chest, I look down the dark hill to the city lights. Out there Heather has lived her entire life. Though I may stay here only a short while each year, I feel like I've grown up here, too. I exhale a deep breath.

"What's the matter?" Heather asks.

I look up at her. "There may not be another year."

She looks at me with a furrowed brow but doesn't speak.

"They won't say it to me," I tell her, "but I've overheard my parents discussing this for a while. They might not be able to justify coming down here another season."

Now Heather looks out at the town.

From this high up, when the season gets under way and all the lights go on, it's easy to spot our Christmas tree lot. Starting tomorrow, a rectangle of white lights will surround our trees. But tonight, the place where I live is a dark patch near a long street with headlights driving past.

"This year will tell us for sure," I say. "I know my parents want to be here as much as I do. Rachel and Elizabeth, on the other hand, love the idea of me staying in Oregon for Christmas."

Heather sits down on the dirt beside me. "You're one of my best friends, Sierra. And I know Rachel and Elizabeth feel the same way, so I can't blame them—but they get you the whole rest of the year. I can't imagine you and your family not being a part of my holidays."

I really don't want to miss my last full season with Heather, either. It's something we've known was coming from the beginning. We've talked about senior year with such apprehensive anticipation.

"I feel the same way," I tell her. "I mean, I am curious

about what the holidays would be like back home—not dealing with school online and getting to do Decemberish things in my hometown for once."

Heather looks up at the stars for a long time.

"But I would miss you," I say, "and all of this way too much."

I see her smile. "Maybe I could come up there for a few days, visit *you* over the break for once."

I lean my head against her shoulder and look out. Not up at the stars or down at the town, but away.

Heather leans her head against mine. "Let's not worry about it right now," she says, and neither of us say anything more for several minutes.

Eventually, I turn back to the smallest tree. I pat the soil around it and slide some more dirt toward its thin trunk. "Let's make this year extra special no matter what," I say.

Heather stands up and looks out at the town. I take her hand and she helps me up. I stand beside her, not letting go.

"What would be amazing," she says, "is if we put lights on these trees so they could be seen by everyone down there."

It's a beautiful thought, a way to share our friendship with everyone. I could open the curtains over my bed and look up at them every night to fall asleep.

"But I checked on the hike up," she says. "This mountain doesn't have a single electrical outlet."

I laugh. "The nature in this town is so behind the times."

CHAPTER FIVE

With my eyes still closed, I hear Mom and Dad shut the door as they leave the trailer. I roll onto my back and take a deep breath. A few extra moments are all I want. Once I get out of bed, the days will tumble forward like dominoes.

On opening day, Mom always wakes up ready to go. I'm much more like Dad, and I can hear his heavy boots on the dirt outside, shuffling toward the Bigtop. Once there, he'll plug in a large silver urn of coffee and one of hot water, and then arrange the packets of tea and powdered chocolate that we put out for customers. The first hot drops of coffee will be poured into his thermos, though.

I pull the tube-shaped pillow from under my head and hug it against my chest. After Heather's mom competes in the ugly Christmas sweater contest, which she's won twice in the past six years, she cuts off the sleeves and makes them into bolster pillows. She sews up the cuff end, stuffs the sleeve with cotton, and then sews up the other end. She keeps one sleeve for her family and the other one goes to me.

I hold the one I got last night at arm's length above me. It's a mossy green fabric with a dark blue rectangle where the elbow was. Within that rectangle, snowflakes fall around a flying purple-nosed reindeer.

I cuddle the pillow tight and close my eyes again. Outside, I hear someone moving toward the trailer.

"Is Sierra around?" Andrew asks.

"Not right now," Dad says.

"Oh, okay," Andrew says. "I figured we could work together and get things done faster."

I squeeze the pillow even tighter. I do not need Andrew waiting outside for me.

"I believe she's still sleeping," Dad says. "But if you need something to do by yourself, double-check the outhouses for hand sanitizer."

That's my dad!

I stand outside the Bigtop, still not fully awake but ready to welcome our first customers of the year. A father and his daughter, who's maybe seven years old, step out of their car. Already scanning the trees, he places a gentle hand on her head.

"I always love this smell," the father says.

The girl takes a step forward, her eyes full of sweet innocence. "It smells like Christmas!"

It smells like Christmas. This is what so many people say when they first arrive, as if the words were waiting to be spoken the entire drive over.

Dad appears from between two noble firs on his way to the Bigtop, probably hoping for more coffee. First, he greets the family and tells them to let any of us know if we can help. Andrew, in a tattered Bulldogs baseball cap, walks by with a watering hose draped over his shoulder. He tells the family he'll be happy to carry a tree to their car when they're ready. He doesn't even glance in at me—thanks to Dad—and I bite down on a grin.

"Is your cash drawer ready?" Dad asks, refilling his thermos.

I walk behind the checkout counter, which has been draped in shiny red garland and fresh holly. "Just waiting to see what the first sell will be."

Dad hands me my favorite mug, painted with pastel squiggles and stripes like an Easter egg (I figure there should be something around here that's not Christmassy). I pour in some coffee and then tear open a packet of powdered chocolate and dump it in. Then I unwrap a small peppermint candy cane and use it to mix it all together.

Dad leans his back against the counter, surveying the merchandise in the Bigtop. He points his thermos at the snow-white trees he finished spraying this morning. "Do you think we have enough of these for now?"

I lick chocolate powder from the thinning candy cane and then drop it back into the mug. "We have plenty," I say, and then I take my first sip. It may taste like a cheap peppermint mocha, but it works.

Eventually, that first father and daughter come into the Bigtop and stop at the cash register.

I lean over the counter toward the little girl. "Did you find a tree you like?"

She nods enthusiastically, a tooth adorably missing from the top of her smile. "A huge one!"

It's our first sale of the year and I can't suppress my excitement, along with a deep-rooted hope that we'll do well enough this year to justify at least one more.

The father slides a tree tag across the counter to me. Behind him, I can see Andrew pushing their tree, trunk first, through the open end of a large plastic barrel. At the other end is a screen of red-and-white netting. Dad grabs the trunk and pulls the rest of the tree out with the netting, which unfurls and wraps around the branches. Once through, the branches are all folded safely upward. Dad and Andrew twist the tree in the netting, cut the end free, and tie a knot at the top. The process is similar to how Heather's mom stuffs her sweater sleeves to make pillows, except way less ugly.

I ring up our first tree and wish them both a "Merry Christmas!"

🎄

At lunch, my legs are tired and achy from loading trees and standing behind the register for hours on end. In a few days, I'll be more used to this, but today I'm grateful when Heather shows up holding a bag of Thanksgiving leftovers. Mom shoos us off into the Airstream, and the first thing Heather does when we sit at the table is open the curtains wide.

She lifts her eyebrows at me. "Just improving the view."

As if on cue, two guys from the baseball team walk by carrying a large tree on their shoulders.

"You have no shame." I unwrap a turkey-and-cranberry sandwich. "Remember, you're still with Devon until after Christmas."

She pulls up her feet to sit cross-legged on the bench, also known as my bed, and unwraps her own sandwich. "He called last night and went into this twenty-minute story about going to the post office."

"So he's not a great conversationalist," I say. I take the first bite of my sandwich and practically hum when the Thanksgiving flavors hit my tongue.

"You don't understand. He told me that same story last week and it was just as pointless then." When I laugh, she throws her hands in the air. "I'm serious! I don't care about that grumpy old lady in front of him trying to ship a box of oysters to Alaska. Would you?"

"Would I ship oysters to Alaska?" I lean forward and tug at the end of her hair. "You're being mean."

"I'm being honest. But if you want to talk about mean," she says, "you dumped that one guy because he liked you *too* much. Talk about soul crushing."

"Mason? That's because he was needy!" I say. "He talked about taking a train ride down here to visit me for the holidays.

That was at the beginning of summer, and we'd only been dating a few weeks."

"It's kind of sweet," Heather says. "He already knew he couldn't do without you for a month. I could definitely use a break from Devon's stories for a month."

When Heather first started dating Devon, she was infatuated with him, and that was only a couple of months ago.

"Anyway," she says, "that's why we need to go on double dates while you're here. It can be casual; you don't need to fall in love or anything."

"Well, that's good to know," I say. "Thank you."

"But at least I'd have someone else to talk to," she says.

"I don't mind being the third wheel when you two go out," I say. "I'll even cut in if he brings up oysters. But this year has me stressed enough without adding some guy into the mix."

Through the window and several trees away, Andrew and another guy from the team are looking at us. They're talking and laughing but don't stop or look away even when we notice them.

"Are they watching us eat?" I ask. "That is so sad."

Andrew glances back over his shoulder, probably checking for my dad, and then waves at us. Before I can decide whether or not to wave back, Dad shouts at them to get to work. I take that opportunity to slide the curtains shut.

Heather's eyebrows are raised. "Well, *he* still seems interested."

I shake my head. "Look, it doesn't matter who the guy is, it would be nothing but trouble with my dad helicoptering over us the entire time. Is there any guy worth that? Because it's not anyone outside this window."

Heather drums her fingers on the tabletop. "It has to be someone who doesn't work here . . . someone your dad can't put on outhouse duty."

"Did you miss where I said I don't want to date while I'm here?"

"I didn't miss it," Heather says, "I'm ignoring it."

Of course she is. "Okay, for the sake of argument let's say I am interested in someone—which I'm not. What type of guy do you think I would attract, knowing I'll be out of his life in a month?"

"You don't have to bring it up," Heather says. "It's obviously a part of the deal, and a month is already longer than some couples last. So don't worry about it. Consider it a holiday love affair."

"'Holiday love affair'? Did you really just say that?" I roll my eyes. "You need to stay away from the Hallmark Channel this time of year."

"Think about it! It's a no-pressure relationship because the whole thing has an end date. And you'll have a great story to tell your friends back home."

I can tell I'm not going to win this one. Heather is more unrelenting than Rachel, which is saying a lot. The only way out is to put things off until it's no longer a possibility because it's too late.

"I'll think about it," I say.

I hear the familiar laughs of two women outside so I pull aside the curtain and peek out. Two middle-aged women from the Downtown Association, their arms full of posters, walk toward the Bigtop.

I wrap up the rest of my sandwich to take with me, and then I give Heather a hug. "I'll keep my eye out for a holiday Romeo, but I need to get back to work now."

Heather rewraps her sandwich and shoves it into the leftovers bag. She follows me out of the trailer and heads toward her car. "I'll keep an eye out for him, too," she calls back.

The Downtown Association ladies are talking to Mom at the counter when I walk up. The oldest lady, with a long gray braid, holds up a poster featuring a garbage truck strung with Christmas lights. "If you could post a few of these again, the city would really appreciate it. Our holiday parade will be bigger than ever this year! We don't want anybody in the community to miss out."

"Of course," Mom says, and the braided lady sets four posters on the counter. "Sierra will have them up this afternoon."

I duck below the counter to grab the staple gun. Heading out of the Bigtop with the posters, I stifle a laugh as I look them over. I'm not sure a festive garbage truck will drum up a larger crowd, but it does foster a small-town feel.

When I was younger, Heather's family brought me with them to the parade a few times, and I will admit it was sentimental fun. Most holiday parades I see now are on TV, coming out of New York or L.A. They don't often include entries like the Society of Pug Owners, or Friends of the Library, or tractors that blast country music Christmas carols as they roll down the streets. Although I can picture them doing that at the hometown parade back in Oregon.

I hold the last poster against a wooden light pole at the entrance to our lot, punching a staple into each of the top corners. Running my hand to the bottom of the poster, I hear Andrew's voice behind me.

"Need any help?"

My shoulders tense. "I've got it."

I punch two more staples into the bottom corners. I then step back and pretend to study my work long enough for Andrew to move on. When I turn around, I see that he wasn't talking to me, but to a gorgeous guy around our age a couple of inches taller than Andrew. The guy holds a tree upright with one hand and wipes his dark hair out of his eyes with the other.

"Thanks, but I'm fine," he says, and Andrew walks away.

The guy looks at me and smiles, a beautiful dimple digging into his left cheek. I can feel my face instantly flush, so I lower my gaze to the dirt. My stomach flutters, and I take a deep breath and remind myself that a cute smile means absolutely nothing about the person.

"Do you work here?" His voice is soft, reminding me of the old crooner songs my grandparents played during the holidays.

I look up, willing myself to act professional. "Did you find everything you need?"

His smile remains, along with that dimple. I brush some hair behind my ears and force myself not to look away. I have to hold myself back from taking a step closer.

"I did," he says. "Thank you."

The way he looks at me—almost studying me—makes me flustered. I clear my throat and look away, but when I look back, he's already walking off, the tree hoisted onto his shoulder like it weighs almost nothing.

"That's a nice shade of red, Sierra."

Standing beside the light pole, Andrew shakes his head at me. I want to respond with something sarcastic, but my tongue hasn't untied yet.

"Did you know dimples are actually a deformity?" he continues. "It means he has a muscle in his face that grew too short. It's kind of gross if you think about it."

I put my weight on one foot and give Andrew my best *Are we done here yet?* look. This maybe comes across as meaner than I'd like to be, but an anvil clearly needs to be dropped on his head if he thinks this kind of jealousy is the way to my heart.

I take the staple gun back to the counter and wait. Maybe the guy with the dimple will return for some tinsel or one of our watering cans with an extra-long spout. Or maybe he needs lights or mistletoe. But then I feel dumb. I told Heather all the reasons I don't want to get involved with anyone while I'm here—good reasons—and those reasons have not changed in the last ten minutes. I'm here for a month. One month! I do not have time, nor the heart, to get involved.

Still, the idea has now taken hold. Maybe I wouldn't mind a little expiration dating. Maybe I wouldn't be so fussy, as my friends like to say, about imperfections if I knew I wouldn't— I couldn't—be with him for more than a few weeks. If he happens to be hot with an adorable dimple, well then, good for him! And me.

I send a text to Heather that afternoon: **What exactly would a holiday love affair entail?**

CHAPTER SIX

The sun has barely risen, but I have two texts waiting for me when I wake up.

The first is from Rachel, complaining about the amount of work it takes to plan a winter formal when sane people are either cramming for finals or holiday shopping. If I were there, I know she would easily convince me to help, but there's not much I can do from nine hundred miles away. Thankfully, balancing my work on the lot with schoolwork isn't too difficult. My teachers send class notes and visuals, and I do the assignments when things slow down and I can hop online. Talking to Monsieur Cappeau once a week won't be the most fun thing in the world, but at least I won't fall out of practice for the oral part of my French grade.

Sitting on my bed, I read the second text from Heather: **Please say you're serious about a holiday boyfriend. Devon** spent the whole night talking about his fantasy football team. Save me! I'm about to make him need a fantasy girlfriend.

I stand up, texting: A really cute guy bought a tree yesterday.

As I'm on my way to take a shower she responds: Details!

Before I can untie the knot on my drawstring pajama bottoms, she texts again: Never mind! Tell me when I bring lunch.

After the shower, I put on a gray sweatshirt and jeans. I pull my hair into a high ponytail, tug out a few strands so they're loose around my face, add a bit of makeup, and then step out into the cool morning. In the Bigtop, Mom stands behind the counter putting change in the register. When she sees me, she points at my still-steaming Easter egg mug on the counter, with a candy cane already sticking out.

"Have you been up long?" I ask.

She blows gently across the surface of her own drink. "Not everyone can sleep through those texts pinging on your phone."

"Oh. Sorry about that."

Dad walks over and kisses us both on the cheek. "Morning."

"Sierra and I were talking about her text messages," Mom says. "I suppose she doesn't need her beauty sleep, but—"

Dad gives her a kiss on the lips. "You don't need it either, honey."

Mom laughs. "Who said I was talking about me?"

Dad scratches the graying stubble along his jaw. "We did agree it's important for her to stay connected to her friends back home."

I decide not to tell them one of the texts was from Heather.

"That's true," Mom says, and then shoots me a look. "But maybe ask your life back home to sleep in occasionally."

I imagine Rachel and Elizabeth right now, probably on the phone planning the rest of this long Thanksgiving weekend.

"Since you brought up life back home," I say, "I think it's time you told me whether or not we're coming back next year."

Mom blinks and rears back her head. She looks at Dad.

Dad takes a long drink from his thermos. "Eavesdropping on our conversations?"

I twist a loose strand of hair. "I wasn't eavesdropping, I *overheard* your conversations," I clarify. "So how worried should I be?"

Dad takes another sip before answering. "There's no reason to worry about the farm," he says. "People will always want Christmas trees, even if they buy them at a superstore. We just may not be selling them ourselves."

Mom touches my arm, an uneasy look on her face. "We will do everything we can to keep the lot open."

"It's not only me I'm concerned about," I say. "Of course I want it to stay open for personal reasons, but this place has been here since Grandpa opened it. It's where the two of you met. It's your life."

Dad nods slowly and ultimately shrugs. "The farm is our life, really. I guess with all the early mornings and late nights back home, I've always seen this as the prize. Watching people get excited about finding the right trees. It'll be hard to let that go."

I admire so much that they've never let this become just a business.

"All that will still be happening with our trees," Dad says, "somewhere, but . . ."

But someone else will get to watch it happen.

Mom drops her hand from my arm and we both look at Dad. This would be the hardest for him.

"The lot has barely broken even the past few years," he says. "Last year, with the bonuses I gave to the crew, we actually lost money. We made up for it with the wholesalers, and I guess that's where things are turning. Your Uncle Bruce has been really focusing on that while we're gone." He takes another sip. "I'm not sure how much we can handle before we finally admit . . ."

He trails off, unable to say it—or unwilling to say it.

"So this might be it," I say. "Our last Christmas in California."

Mom's face is a mirror of gentleness. "We haven't decided anything, Sierra. But it might be a good idea to make this one memorable."

Heather steps into the trailer carrying two more bags of leftovers. Her eyes are electric, and I know she wants me to dish on the cute guy who came by yesterday. Devon walks in after her, looking at his phone. Even with his face bowed, I can tell he's good-looking.

"Sierra, this is Devon. Devon, this is . . . Devon, look up."

He looks up at me and smiles. His short brown hair frames round cheeks, but it's his comforting eyes that make me like him immediately.

"It's nice to meet you," I say.

"You too," he says. He holds my gaze long enough to prove his sincerity, and then his face dives back into his phone.

Heather hands Devon one of the bags of food. "Baby, go bring this to the guys out there. And then help them out loading trees or something."

Devon takes the bag without glancing up from his phone and then leaves the trailer. Heather sits across from me at the table, and I move my computer onto the pillow beside me.

"I'm guessing your parents weren't home when Devon picked you up," I say. Heather looks confused, so I point at her hair. "It's a little messy in back."

Her cheeks go red and she rakes her fingers through the tangles. "Oh, right . . ."

"So are things looking up between you and Mr. Monosyllabic?"

"That's a nice word," she says. "If the choice is between listening to him or kissing him, kissing is a much better use of his mouth."

I burst out laughing.

"I know, I know, I'm a horrible human being," she says. "So tell me about that guy who came in."

"I have no idea who he is. There's not much to say."

"What does he look like?" Heather pops the lid off a

container of turkey salad, which has walnut and celery chunks. Her family is still trying to rid their house of Thanksgiving.

"I only saw him for a moment," I say, "but he looked about our age. He had this dimple that—"

Heather leans forward, her eyes narrowed. "And dark hair? A killer smile?"

How does she know that?

Heather pulls out her phone, taps it a few times, and then shows me an online picture of the very guy I was talking about. "Is this him?" She does not look pleased.

"How did you know?"

"The first thing you mentioned was his dimple. That was the giveaway." She shakes her head. "Plus, that would be my luck. Sorry, Sierra, but no. Not Caleb."

So his name is Caleb. "Why?"

She leans back and sets her fingertips on the edge of the tabletop. "He's just not the best choice, okay? Let's find someone else."

I'm not letting this stop here and she knows it.

"There's this rumor," she says, "but I'm pretty sure it's true. Either way, something happened."

"What is it?" This is the first time I've heard her speak so cryptically of someone. "You're making me nervous."

She shakes her head. "I don't want to get into this. I hate being a gossip, but I am not going on a double date with him."

"Tell me."

"It's unconfirmed, okay? It's only what I've heard." She

looks me in the eyes, but I am not saying a word until I hear it. "They say he attacked his sister with a knife."

"What?" My stomach twists. "That guy is . . . Is she still alive?"

Heather laughs, but I can't tell if it's from my shocked expression or because she was joking. My heart still pounds, but eventually I laugh a little, too.

"No, he didn't murder her," Heather says. "From what I know, she's fine."

So it wasn't a joke.

"But she doesn't live here anymore," Heather says. "I don't know if that's because of the attack, but that's what most people think."

I lie down on my bed and place a hand over my forehead. "That is intense."

Heather reaches under the table and pats my leg. "We'll keep looking."

I want to tell her not to bother. I want to tell her I'm not interested in a holiday love affair anymore, especially if my radar is so off that the one guy I picked out once attacked his sister with a knife.

After we finish the turkey salad, we go outside to round up Devon so I can head back to work. He's sitting at a picnic table behind the Bigtop with a bunch of the guys, all picking through Heather's leftovers. There's also a pretty girl I've never seen, snuggling up close to Andrew.

"I don't think we've met," I say. "I'm Sierra."

"Oh, your parents own this place!" She holds out a manicured hand and I shake it. "I'm Alyssa. I just stopped by to meet Andrew for lunch."

I glance at Andrew, who is now three shades of red.

He shrugs. "We're not . . . you know . . ."

The girl's face drops. Her hand covers her heart and she looks at Andrew. "Are you two . . . ?"

"No!" I say quickly.

I'm not sure what Andrew's trying to do. If he is with her, does he want me to think it's not serious? Like I care! Anyway, I hope they become serious. Maybe Alyssa will help him get over whatever he holds for me.

I turn to Heather. "Will I see you later?"

"Devon and I can pick you up after you close," she says. "Maybe we'll go out and try to meet some people—or *someone*. You only want one, right?"

Heather is not only pushy, she doesn't even attempt to be subtle.

She raises an eyebrow at me. "One month, Sierra. A lot can happen in a month."

"Not tonight," I say. "Maybe soon."

But for the next few days, I can't stop thinking about Caleb.

CHAPTER SEVEN

On most weekdays, Heather stops by on her way home from school. Sometimes she hangs out at the counter and helps me out when parents show up with young children. While I ring up the mom or dad, she distracts the kids.

"Last night, I asked Devon what he wanted for Christmas," Heather says from the drink station. She's carefully putting mini-marshmallows, one by one, into her hot chocolate.

"What did he say?"

"Hold on, I'm counting." After she places her eighteenth marshmallow, she takes a sip. "He shrugged. That was the extent of the conversation. So I figured, it's probably for the best. What if he wanted something expensive? Then if he asked me, *I'd* have to say something expensive."

"And that's a problem because . . ."

"I can't have us buying nice things for each other right before I break up with him!"

"So you can both make something," I say. "Something small and inexpensive."

"Homemade and thoughtful? That's worse!" She walks to a flocked tree and gently touches the fake snow. "How do you break up with someone who just carved you a wooden figurine or something?"

"This is getting way too complicated," I say. From beneath the counter, I pull out a cardboard box full of bagged mistletoe and set it on the stool. "Maybe you should do it now. He's going to get hurt either way."

"No, I'm definitely keeping him through the holidays." Taking another sip, she approaches the opposite side of the counter. "But it's time to get serious about picking someone for you. The parade is coming up and I want you to double with us."

I reach across the counter to restock the mistletoe display. "I'm thinking this whole idea of a holiday romance isn't going to work. I will admit I did consider it when I saw Caleb, but first impressions are clearly not my strength."

Heather looks me straight in the eyes and nods toward the parking lot. "Remember that, okay? Because here he comes."

I can feel my eyes go wide.

She takes a step back and motions for me to come join her. I walk around the counter and she points to an old purple pickup truck. The cab is empty.

If that is his truck, what's he doing here? He already

bought a tree. Below the tailgate is a bumper sticker for a school I've never heard of.

"Where's Sagebrush Junior High?" I ask.

Heather shrugs, and a curl falls loose from where she had it tucked behind her ear.

This city has six elementary schools. Each winter I went to the same one as Heather. Those feed into the one middle school, which I also went to, and then one high school. That's when I started doing my assignments online.

Heather looks into the trees. "Oh! There he is. God, he's cute."

"I know," I whisper. I avoid where she's looking and instead watch the toe of my shoe dig into the dirt.

She touches my elbow and whispers, "Here he comes." Before I can say anything, she makes a beeline to the far side of the Bigtop.

From the corner of my eye, I see someone emerge from between two of our trees. Caleb walks straight toward me, shining his dimpled smile. "Is your name Sierra?"

All I can do is nod.

"So you're the one the workers are talking about."

"Excuse me?"

He laughs once. "I didn't know if there was maybe some other girl working today."

"Just me," I say. "My parents own this place. And run it."

"Now it makes sense why they're afraid to talk to you," he says. When I don't respond, he continues, "I was here the other day. You asked if I needed help?"

I don't know what I should say. He shifts his weight between his feet. When I still don't say anything, he shifts his weight again, which almost makes me laugh. At least I'm not the only one who's nervous.

Behind him, I see two of the baseball players sweeping up needles between the trees.

Caleb steps beside me and watches them sweep. I hold still, forcing myself not to move away. "Does your dad really make them clean outhouses if they talk to you?"

"Even if he *thinks* they want to talk to me."

"Then your outhouses must be extremely clean," he says, which is the weirdest pickup line I've ever heard, if that's what that was.

"Can I help you with something?" I ask. "I know you already have a tree . . ."

"So you do remember me." He seems a little too pleased by this.

"I do the inventory," I say, flipping the memory of him into pure business, "and I'm good at my job."

"I see." He nods slowly. "What kind of tree did I get?"

"A noble fir." I have no idea if that's true.

Now he seems impressed.

I walk around the counter, putting the cash register and mistletoe between us. "Anything else we can help you with?"

He hands me a tag from a tree. "This one's bigger than the last, so a couple of the guys are putting it in my truck right now."

I find myself staring into his eyes for too long, so I wrench my gaze to the nearest displays. "Do you need a wreath to go with it? They're fresh. Or an ornament?" Part of me wants to just sell him the tree so he can leave and this awkwardness will end, but part of me also wants him to stay.

He doesn't say anything for several seconds, which forces me to look at him again, and he's scanning everything inside the Bigtop. Maybe he does need something else. Or maybe he's looking for an excuse to stay longer. Then, when he sees the drinks, his smile gets brighter. "I'll definitely take a hot chocolate."

At the drink station, he lifts a paper cup from the top of the upside-down cup tower. Beyond him, I see Heather peek out from behind a flocked tree, sipping on her own hot chocolate. When she sees me watching, she shakes her head and mouths "Bad idea" before slowly sliding herself back behind the branches.

My heart skips a beat when he unwraps a candy cane to stir the chocolate powder in his hot water. When he lets go of the candy cane, it continues spinning in the swirling drink.

"That's how I make mine," I say.

"Why wouldn't you?"

"It's like a cheap peppermint mocha," I tell him.

He tilts his head and looks at his drink with new eyes. "You could call it that, but that sounds kind of insulting." He passes the drink to his other hand and then reaches across the counter to shake.

"Nice to officially meet you, Sierra."

I look at his hand, then at him, and hesitate for a split

second. In that moment, I see his shoulders deflate a bit. I know better than to be so judgmental over a rumor even Heather wasn't sure of. I shake his hand. "You're Caleb, right?"

His smile falters. "So someone told you about me."

I freeze. Even if he isn't the guy I'll have a holiday romance with, he doesn't deserve to be second-guessed by someone who only recently learned his name. "I must have overheard your name from someone who helped you," I say.

He smiles, but his dimple doesn't appear. "So, how much do I owe you?"

I ring him up and he pulls out his wallet, which is stuffed thick with bills. He hands me two twenties and a whole lot of ones.

"I didn't get to cash out my tips from last night," he says, a slight blush rising. The dimple pushes deep into his cheek again.

It takes pure willpower not to ask where he works so I can accidentally on purpose drop by. "We can always use more ones," I say. I count out the singles and hand him back fifty cents in change.

He puts the coins in his pocket and the blush disappears, his confidence back. "Maybe I'll see you some more before Christmas."

"You know where to find me," I say. I'm not sure if that came across as an invitation, or if maybe that is exactly how I meant it. Do I want to see him again? It's not my business to figure out his story, but I can't stop picturing the way his shoulders dropped when I didn't shake his hand right away.

He heads out of the Bigtop, slipping the wallet into his back pocket. Giving him a moment, I then creep out from behind the counter to watch him leave. As he walks up to his truck, he hands a few dollars to one of the guys.

Heather steps beside me and we watch as Caleb and one of our workers shut the tailgate together.

"From my perspective, that looked awkward for both of you," she says. "I'm sorry, Sierra. I shouldn't have said anything."

"No, there's something there," I say. "I don't know how much is true, but that guy's carrying some sort of baggage."

She looks at me with a vaulted eyebrow. "You're still into him, aren't you? You're actually thinking about getting involved."

I laugh and return to my station behind the counter. "He's cute. That's all. It's not enough for me to get involved."

"Well, that's very wise," Heather says, "but he is the only guy I've seen you this awkward around since I've known you."

"He was awkward, too!"

"He had his moments," she says, "but you won that contest."

🌲

After a phone call where I describe my week in French to Monsieur Cappeau, Mom lets me leave work early. Heather holds a movie marathon every year starring her latest celebrity crush and a bottomless bowl of popcorn. Dad offers me his truck, but I decide to walk. Back home I would have grabbed his keys in a second to avoid the cold. Here, even in late November, it's relatively nice out.

The walk takes me past the only other family-owned tree lot in town. Their assortment of trees and the red-and-white sales tent take up three rows of a supermarket parking lot. I always stop by a couple of times during the season to say hi. Like my parents, the Hoppers rarely leave their spot once the selling begins.

With his arms buried into the top half of a tree, Mr. Hopper leads a customer into the parking lot. I walk toward them, squeezing between parked cars, to say hello for the first time this year. The guy carrying the trunk of the tree drops his end onto the lowered tailgate of a purple truck.

Caleb?

Mr. Hopper pushes the tree the rest of the way in. He turns in my direction and I don't spin away fast enough. "Sierra?"

I exhale deeply and then turn back around. Wearing a checkered orange-and-black jacket and matching earflapped hat, Mr. Hopper walks over and embraces me in a warm hug. I use that squeeze to look over at Caleb. He leans his back against the truck and his eyes smile at me.

Mr. Hopper and I catch up quickly and I agree to stop by some more before Christmas. When he heads back to his lot, Caleb is still looking at me, sipping something from a paper cup with a lid.

"Tell me what your addiction is," I say. "Is it the Christmas trees or the hot drinks?"

His dimple digs in deep and I walk closer. His hair sticks up in front, like all this tree lifting doesn't allow him enough time to brush it. Before he answers my question, Mr. Hopper and one of the workers drop a second tree into Caleb's truck.

Caleb looks at me and shrugs.

"Seriously, what is going on?" I ask.

He nonchalantly lifts the tailgate shut as if finding him at another tree lot isn't extremely odd. "I'd like to know what brings *you* here?" he asks. "Are you checking out the competition?"

"Oh, there's no competition at Christmastime," I say. "But since you do appear to be an expert, who's got the best lot?"

He takes a sip of his drink and I watch his Adam's apple bob as he swallows it down. "Your family has them beat," he says. "These guys were all out of candy canes."

I feign disgust. "How dare they."

"I know!" he says. "Maybe I should stick with you guys."

He takes another sip, followed by silence. Is he implying there will be even more trees? That means more opportunities to run into him, and I don't know how I should feel about that.

"What kind of person buys this many trees in a day?" I ask. "Or even in a season?"

"To answer your first question," he says, "I'm addicted to the hot chocolate. I suppose if I have to have an addiction, it's not the worst one. To your second question, when you own a truck, you end up with plenty of ways to fill it. For example, I helped three people my mom works with move over the summer."

"I see. So you're that guy," I say. I walk up to one of his trees and pull gently on the needles. "You're the one everyone can count on for help."

He rests his arms on the wall of his truck bed. "Does that surprise you?"

He's testing me because he knows I've heard something about him. And he's right to test me, because I'm not sure how to answer. "Should it surprise me?"

He looks down at his trees, and I can tell he's disappointed that I dodged the question.

"I assume these trees aren't all for you," I say.

He smiles.

I lean forward, not sure if I should be doing this, but also feeling compelled. "Well, if you plan to buy any more, I know the owners at the other lot fairly well. I think I can get you a discount."

He takes out his wallet, again stuffed with one-dollar bills, and pulls out a few singles. "Actually, I've been there two times since I saw you hanging that parade sign, but you were out."

Was that an admission that he had hoped to see me? I can't ask that, of course, so I point to his wallet. "You know, banks will let you exchange all those ones for something bigger."

He turns the wallet over in his hands. "What can I say, I'm lazy."

"At least you know your flaws," I say. "That's healthy."

He shoves the wallet in his pocket. "Knowing my flaws is one thing I'm good at."

If I were bolder, I would use that as an opening to ask about his sister, but a question like that could so easily send him into his truck, driving away.

"Flaws, huh?" I take a step closer to him. "Buying all these trees and helping people move, you must be at the top of Santa's naughty list."

"If you put it that way, I guess I'm not all bad."

I snap my fingers. "You probably consider your sweet tooth a major sin."

"No, I don't remember that one being mentioned in church," he says. "But laziness has been, and I am that. I still haven't replaced the comb I lost a few months ago."

"And look at the results," I say, eyeing his hair. "That's almost unforgivable. You may need to peruse elsewhere for discounted trees."

"*Peruse?*" he says. "I mean, it's a good word, but I don't think I've used it in a sentence before."

"Oh, please don't tell me you consider that a big word."

He laughs, and his laugh is so perfect I want to continue drawing it out of him. But this comfort in our teasing isn't good. Regardless of how cute he is, or easy to joke with, I have to remember Heather's concern.

As if he can see the thoughts turning in my mind, his face turns resentful. His gaze falls back to the trees. "What?" he asks.

If we keep running into each other, there will always be a conversation—this rumor—hanging over us.

"Look, obviously I heard something . . ." The words dry up in my throat. But why do I need to say them? We can just go back to being the customer and the tree girl. This does not need to come up.

"You're right, it's very obvious," he says. "It always is."

"But I don't want to believe it if—"

He pulls his keys out of his pocket and still won't look at me. "Then don't worry about it. We can be nice to each other, I'll buy my trees from you, but . . ." His jaw clenches. I can tell he's trying to raise his eyes to look at me, but he can't.

There is nothing more I can say. He hasn't told me that what I've heard is a lie. The next words need to come from him.

He moves to the cab of his truck, gets in, and pulls the door shut.

I step back.

He starts the engine and then gives me a small wave as he drives off.

CHAPTER EIGHT

I don't start work until noon on Saturday, so Heather picks me up early and I ask her to take us to Breakfast Express. She looks at me strangely but drives in that direction.

"Did you find out if you can go to the parade with us?" she asks.

"It shouldn't be a problem," I say. "The whole town goes to that thing. We won't be swamped until after it ends."

I think about the sad wave Caleb offered when he drove off last night and the weight on his shoulders that kept him from looking at me. Even if there are reasons not to get involved, I still want to see his truck drive up to the lot again.

"Devon thinks you should ask Andrew to the parade," Heather says. "Now, I know what you're going to say . . ."

I'm thankful my eyeballs don't pop out onto her dash-board. "Did you tell Devon that's a terrible idea?"

She lifts a shoulder. "He thinks you should give him a chance. I'm not saying I agree with him, but Andrew does like you."

"Well, I completely don't like him." I scrunch down in my seat. "Wow. That sounded so mean."

Heather pulls up to the curb in front of Breakfast Express, a 1950s-themed diner housed in two retired train cars. One car is the diner and the other is the kitchen. Beneath both cars, the steel wheels are anchored to actual rails set over splintered wooden ties. Best of all, they serve breakfast—*only* breakfast—all day long.

Before she turns off the engine, Heather looks past me to the windows of the train cars. "Look, I wasn't going to say no to this because I know you love coming here."

"Okay," I say, unsure what that was all about. "If you want to go somewhere else—"

"But before we go in," she says, "you should know that Caleb works here." She waits for that to sink in, and it sinks down like a rock.

"Oh."

"I don't know if he's working today, but he may be," she says. "So figure out how you're going to be."

While approaching the stairs to the diner car, my heart beats faster and faster the closer I get. I follow Heather up the steps, and she pulls open the red metal door.

Vinyl records and photos from old movies and TV shows decorate the walls up to the ceiling. The center aisle is lined on either side with tables that can seat no more than four, and plastic red cushions flecked with silver sparkles. Only three tables are occupied right now.

"Maybe he won't be here," I say. "Maybe it's his day—"

Before I can finish, the door to the kitchen slides open and Caleb walks through. He's wearing a white button-down shirt, khakis, and a paper soda jerk hat. He carries a serving tray with two breakfast plates to a table and then sets one plate in front of each person. He lowers the tray to his side and then makes his way toward us. After a few steps, he blinks with recognition, his gaze moving between Heather and me. His smile appears cautious, but at least it's there.

I stuff my hands into my coat pockets. "Caleb. I didn't know you worked here."

He grabs two menus from a shelf beside Heather, his smile fading. "Would you have come if you did?"

I don't know how to answer.

"This was her favorite place as a kid," Heather says.

"It's true," I say. "The silver dollar pancakes were my favorite."

Caleb starts walking down the aisle. "No need to explain."

Heather and I follow him to a table at the far end of the car. Like every booth we pass, it has its own rectangular window. On this side, the windows look out onto the street where we parked.

"It's the best booth in the train," he says.

Heather and I slide into the booth on opposite sides of the table.

"What makes it so great?" I ask.

67

"It's closest to the kitchen." His smile returns. "A fresh pot of coffee will get to you before anyone else. Plus, it makes it easier to chat with people I know."

At that, Heather picks up a menu and starts reading it over. Without looking away, she slides the other menu closer to me. I can't tell if that was meant to look dismissive to Caleb, but it did.

"If you get bored," I tell him, "we'll be here."

Caleb looks at Heather as she continues reading her menu. No one speaks for several seconds, and then Caleb concedes and disappears behind the kitchen door.

I push Heather's menu to the table. "What was that? I'm sure now he thinks you're the one who told me the rumor. But you don't even know if it's true."

"I don't know how *much* of it is true," she says. "I'm sorry, I just didn't know what to say. I'm worried for you."

"Why? Because I think he's cute? As far as I know that's all he's got going for him."

"But he's interested in you, Sierra. I see him every day at school and he's never this talkative. And that's fine, but you don't have to be so obviously flirting back when—"

"Whoa!" I hold up a hand. "First of all, I was not obviously anything. Second, I don't even know him, so there's no reason for you to worry."

Heather picks up her menu again, but I can tell she's not reading it.

"Here's what I do know about Caleb," I say. "He works at

a diner and buys a lot of trees. So while I probably will continue running into him, that's where it ends. I don't need to see him more than that, and I don't want to know more than that. Okay?"

"I get it," Heather says. "I'm sorry."

"Good." I sit back. "Then maybe I can enjoy my silver dollar pancakes without this knot in my stomach."

Heather gives me a half-smile. "Those things will *cause* a knot in your stomach."

I pick up my menu and look it over even though I know what I'm getting. This gives me somewhere to look while I push the subject further. "Besides, whatever did happen, he still tortures himself over it."

Heather slaps her menu on the table. "You talked to him about it?"

"We didn't have a chance," I say, "but his whole body showed it."

She looks over at the closed door to the kitchen. When she turns back to me, she presses her palms against her temples. "Why are people so complicated?"

I laugh. "Right? It would be so much easier if they were just like us."

"Okay, before he comes back," Heather says, "here's what I know about him. And it's only what I know for sure—no rumors."

"Perfect."

"Caleb and I have never been friends, but he's never been

anything but nice to me. There must be—or must have *been*—another side, but I've never seen it."

I motion toward her menu. "Then don't be so cold to him."

"I'm not trying to be." She leans forward and puts a hand on top of mine. "I want you to have fun while you're here, but you can't do that if the guy's carrying more baggage than a jumbo jet."

The door slides open and Caleb walks out with a small pad and pencil. He stops beside us.

"Are you hiring?" Heather asks.

Caleb puts down his writing tools. "Are you looking?"

"No, but Devon needs a job," she says. "He refuses to look for one himself, but I know it would spice up his life a little."

"You're his girlfriend," I say with a laugh. "Isn't that *your* job?"

Heather kicks me under the table.

"Or are you trying to get rid of him?" Caleb asks.

"I didn't say that," Heather says a little too fast.

Caleb laughs. "The less I know, the better. But I'll ask my manager when he gets here."

"Thank you," Heather says.

He turns to me. "If you're hoping for hot chocolate, you should know we don't have any candy canes. It might not meet your standards."

"Coffee's fine," I say. "But with tons of cream and sugar."

"I'll take the hot chocolate," Heather says. "Can you add extra marshmallows?"

Caleb nods. "Be right back."

Once he's out of earshot, Heather leans forward. "Did you hear that? He wants to meet your standards."

I lean right back at her. "He's a waiter," I say. "That's his job."

When Caleb returns he's carrying one ceramic mug topped off with an exaggerated pile of marshmallows. He sets it on the table and a few of them spill out.

"Don't worry, I'm brewing more coffee," he tells me.

The door at the other end of the diner opens. When Caleb looks over to see who walked in, a mix of surprise and happiness appears in his eyes. I turn and see a mom with twin girls—maybe six years old—smiling at Caleb. The girls are thin and both wear hooded sweatshirts, tattered at the cuffs and a size too big. One of the girls holds up a crayon drawing of a decorated Christmas tree high enough for Caleb to see.

"I'll be right back," he whispers to us. He walks over to the girls and is presented with the drawing. "It's beautiful. Thank you."

"It's like the tree you gave us," one of the girls says.

"It's all decorated now," the other one tells him. "It looks just like this."

Caleb looks closely at the picture.

"They don't remember the last time they had a tree," the mom says. She adjusts the purse strap on her shoulder. "I barely remember getting one myself. And when they got home from school, their faces . . . they just . . ."

"Thank you for this," Caleb says. He brings the drawing close to his chest. "But it was my pleasure."

The mom takes a deep breath. "The girls wanted to thank you in person."

"We said a prayer for you," one girl says.

Caleb slightly bows his head toward the girl. "That means a lot."

"When we called the food bank, the man said you do this on your own," the mom says. "He told us you worked here and probably wouldn't mind if we stopped by."

"Well, he was right about that. In fact . . ." Caleb steps aside and points to the nearest table. "Would you like some hot chocolates?"

The girls cheer, but the mom says, "We can't stay. We—"

"I'll put them in to-go cups," Caleb says. When the mom doesn't decline, he begins walking in our direction and I turn back to Heather.

When he's in the kitchen, I whisper, "That's why he buys all these trees? To give them to families he doesn't even know?"

"He didn't say anything to you when he bought them?" Heather asks.

I look out the window to the cars passing by. I charged him full price for that first tree and I'm sure Mr. Hopper's doing the same. But here he is working at a diner, buying tree after tree after tree. I'm not sure where to place this new information with the other story I've heard about him.

Caleb returns from the kitchen. In one hand he holds a cardboard carrier with three to-go cups with lids. In the other he has a mug of coffee, which he sets in front of me before continuing on to the family. I stare at Heather as I sip my coffee, already mixed with the perfect combination of cream and sugar.

Eventually Caleb returns and stands beside our table. "Is the coffee okay?" he asks. "I mixed it in back because I couldn't carry their drinks and yours with the cream and sugar."

"It's perfect," I say. Beneath the table, I kick at Heather's shoe. She looks at me and I slightly tilt my head to the side, asking her to scoot over. If I were to ask Caleb to sit beside me, it'd be a definitive sign that I'm interested. If Heather invites him, after already saying she's with Devon, it becomes a mere friendly conversation.

Heather scoots over. "Have a seat, tree boy."

Caleb looks surprised but pleased by the offer. He gives a quick glance to the other tables before sitting across from me.

"You know," Heather says, "it's been a while since anyone gave me a crayon drawing of a Christmas tree."

"I was not expecting that," Caleb says. He sets the drawing in the middle of the table, turning it so it faces me. "It's really good, isn't it?"

I admire the tree, and then I look at him. He's still looking down at the drawing.

"You, Caleb, are a man of multitudes," I say.

Without taking his eyes off the drawing, he says, "I need to point out that you used *multitude* in a sentence."

"It's not the first time," Heather says.

Caleb looks at her. "She may be the first person in this diner to ever use it."

"You—both of you—are ridiculous," I say. "Heather, tell him you've used *peruse* in a sentence before. It's two syllables."

"Of course I . . ." She stops herself and looks at Caleb. "No, actually, I probably never have."

Caleb and Heather bump fists.

I reach over and snatch that silly looking soda jerk hat from Caleb's head. "Then you should use more interesting words, sir. And buy yourself a comb."

He holds out his hand. "My hat, please? Or the next time I buy a tree, I'm paying for it all in one-dollar bills, each one turned a different direction."

"Fine," I say, still holding his hat out of reach.

Caleb stands up, his hand out for his hat, and I eventually give it back. He perches the completely uncool thing back on his head.

"If you do come for a tree, don't expect any drawings," I say, "but I work from noon to eight today."

Heather stares at me, a half-smile appearing on her face. When Caleb leaves to check on the other customers, she says, "You basically just asked him to stop by."

"I know," I say, lifting my mug. "*That* was me obviously flirting."

I get to work an hour before Mom thought I would be needed, which is a good thing. The lot is busy and a flatbed truck full of replenishing trees from the farm arrived early. With my work gloves on I climb up the ladder at the back of the truck. I step carefully onto the top layer of trees, all

74

netted and laid sideways one on top of the other, their wet needles brushing against the bottom of my pants. It must have rained for a good part of the trip, giving the trees a smell that's close to home.

Two more workers join me up here, moving their feet as little as possible to keep the branches from snapping. I lace my fingers into the netting of a tree, bend my knees, and slide it over the edge of the truck so another worker can grab it and carry it to a growing stack behind the Bigtop.

Andrew takes the next tree I lower and, rather than carry it to the Bigtop himself, he passes it off to someone else.

"We got this!" he shouts up to me, clapping his hands twice.

I almost tell him we aren't in a race, but Dad drops his hand on Andrew's shoulder.

"The outhouses need restocking, pronto," he says. "And let me know if you think they need a deeper cleaning. That decision's up to you."

When my muscles start to tire, I take a moment to stretch my back and catch my breath. Even when exhausted, it's easy to keep a smile going on the lot. I look out at the customers moving through our trees, the joy on their faces evident even from way up here.

I've been surrounded by these sights my entire life. Now, I realize that the only people I'm seeing are the ones who *will* have a tree for Christmas. The people I don't see are the families who can't afford a tree even if they want one. Those are the people Caleb brings our trees to.

I put my hands on my hips and twist in both directions. Beyond our lot—beyond the last house in the city—Cardinals Peak rises into the cloudless pale blue sky. Near the top of that hill are my trees, indistinguishable from here.

Dad climbs the ladder to help me slide more trees down to the workers. After lowering a few, he looks at me with his hands on his knees. "Did I react too strongly with Andrew?" he asks.

"Don't worry," I say, "he knows I'm not interested."

Dad lowers another tree, a delighted smile on his face.

I look out over the workers on the lot. "I think everyone here knows I'm off-limits."

He stands up and wipes his wet hands on his jeans. "Honey, I don't think we put too many restrictions on you. Do you?"

"Not at home." I send down another tree. "But here? I don't think you'd be too comfortable with me seeing anyone."

He grips another tree, but then stops to look at me and doesn't pass it over the side. "It's because I know how easy it can be to fall for someone in a very short time. Trust me, leaving like that is not easy."

I lower two more trees and then notice he's still looking at me. "Okay," I say. "I understand."

With the trees finally unloaded, Dad takes off his gloves and shoves them into his back pocket. He heads to the trailer for a short nap and I walk toward the Bigtop to help ring up customers. I pull back my hair to wrap it into a bun when I see, standing at the counter, Caleb in his street clothes.

I let my hair fall to my shoulders and scrape a few strands forward.

I pass him by as I head to the counter. "Back again, making someone else's Christmas bright?"

He smiles. "It's what I do."

I nod for him to follow me to the drink station. Next to my Easter mug I set a paper cup for him and then I tear open a packet of hot chocolate. "So tell me, what made you start doing this with the trees?"

"It's a long story," he says, and his smile falters a bit. "If you'll take the simple version, Christmas was always a big deal in my family."

I know his sister doesn't live with him anymore; maybe that's part of the non-short story. I hand him his cup of hot chocolate with a candy cane stirrer. His dimple reappears when he sees my Easter mug, and we both take a sip while looking at each other.

"My parents would let my sister and me buy whichever tree we wanted," he says. "They'd invite friends over and we'd all decorate the house. We'd cook a pot of chili and afterwards we'd all go caroling. Sounds really cheesy, right?"

I point to the flocked trees around us. "My family *survives* on cheesy Christmas traditions. But that doesn't explain why you buy them for other people."

He takes another sip. "My church does this big 'necessity drive' during the holidays," he says. "We collect things like coats and toothbrushes for families that need them. It's great.

But sometimes it's nice to give people what they want instead of only the necessities."

"I can appreciate that," I say.

He blows steam from the surface of his drink. "My family doesn't do the holidays like we used to. We put up a tree, but that's about it."

I want to ask why, but I'm sure that's also part of the non-simple version.

"Long story short, I took the job at Breakfast Express and realized I could spend my tips on families who wanted a Christmas tree but couldn't afford it." He stirs the peppermint stick. "I guess if I earned more tips, you'd see even more of me."

I sip up a small marshmallow and lick it from my lip. "Maybe you should put out a separate tip jar," I say. "Draw a little tree on it and have a note saying what the money's for."

"I thought about that," he says. "But I like using my money. I'd feel bad if that extra tip somehow took away from a charity that gives people what they actually need."

I set my mug on the counter and point at his hair. "Speaking of things people need, don't move." I run behind the counter for a small paper bag. I hold it out to Caleb and his eyebrows raise.

He takes the bag, looks inside, and laughs so hard when he pulls out the purple comb I picked up for him at the pharmacy.

"It's time to start tackling those flaws," I say.

He slides the comb into his back pocket and thanks me.

Before I can explain that the comb is first supposed to go through his hair, the Richardson family walks into the Bigtop.

"I was wondering when you'd show up!" I give both Mr. and Mrs. Richardson hugs. "Aren't you normally day-after-Thanksgiving tree buyers?"

The Richardsons are a family of eight who have been buying their trees from us since they only had two children. Every year they bring us a tin of home-baked cookies and chat with me while their kids bicker over which tree is the most perfect. Today, their kids all say hi to me and then run out to start looking.

"There was car trouble on the way to New Mexico," Mr. Richardson says. "We spent Thanksgiving in a motel room waiting for a fan belt to arrive."

"Thank you, God, they had a pool there or the kids would have killed each other." Mrs. Richardson hands me this year's blue snowflake-covered cookie tin. "We tried a new recipe this year. We found it online and everyone swears it's delicious."

I pull off the lid and pick out a slightly misshapen snowman cookie that has a ton of frosting and sprinkles. Caleb's leaning in, so I offer him the tin and he takes a mutated reindeer with buck teeth.

"The younger kids helped out this year," Mr. Richardson says, "which you could probably tell."

I moan around the first bite. "Oh my, yum . . . These are delicious!"

"Enjoy them now," Mrs. Richardson says, "because next year I'm going back to the Pillsbury version."

Caleb catches a crumb falling from his lips. "These are amazing."

"A lady at work says we should try some peppermint bark," Mr. Richardson says. "She says even the kids can't mess it up." He tries to reach into my tin for a cookie, but Mrs. Richardson grabs his elbow and pulls him back.

Caleb snags another cookie and I shoot him a look. "Excuse me! You have now exceeded your allotment." I know he would love to tease me for saying *allotment*, and it is fun to watch him struggle, but he would rather eat the cookie.

"Eat all you want," Mrs. Richardson says. "I can give you and your boyfriend the recipe and—"

Mr. Richardson touches his wife's arm at the word *boyfriend*. I smile at him to let him know it's okay. Besides, one of their children is now screaming outside.

Mrs. Richardson sighs. "It's been lovely seeing you again, Sierra."

Mr. Richardson nods at us both before leaving. Once outside, he shouts, "Santa sees you, Nathan!"

Caleb steals another cookie and pops it in his mouth.

I point at him. "Santa sees you, Caleb."

He holds his hands up innocently and walks to the drink station for a napkin, which he scrubs across his mouth. "You should come with me on tonight's tree run," he says.

I nearly choke on my cookie mid-swallow.

He tosses the crumpled napkin into the green plastic trash can. "You don't have to if—"

"I'd love to," I say. "But I work tonight."

He looks me in the eyes, his expression shallow. "You don't have to make excuses, Sierra. Just be straight with me."

I step toward him. "I work until eight. I told you that, remember?" Is he always this defensive?

He bites his top lip and faces outside. "I know there are things we should talk about," he says, "but not yet, okay? Just, if you can, don't believe everything you hear."

"I *will* go with you another day, Caleb. All right? Very soon." I wait for his eyes to look at me. "Unless *you* don't want me to."

He picks up another napkin to wipe his hands. "I do. I think you'd really like it."

"Good," I say, "because it means a lot that you want me to go."

He stifles a smile, but his dimple gives it away. "You grew the trees. You deserve to see what they bring to these families."

I wave my candy cane toward the trees. "I get to see it every day."

"This is different," he says.

I stir my drink with the candy cane and study the spirals it forms. It feels like this will be more than two people simply hanging out. It feels like I'm being asked out. If he did that, having nothing to do with trees, a part of me would love to say yes. But how much do I honestly know about him? And he knows even less about me.

He pulls out his comb and wags it in front of him. "This isn't getting used until you commit to an exact date."

"Oh, now you're playing rough," I say. "Let me think.

This weekend is going to get real busy here, so I'll be exhausted after work. Can we go Monday when you're done with school?"

He looks up, like he's checking the calendar in his head. "I don't work that day. Let's do it! I'll come get you after dinner."

Caleb and I leave the Bigtop together, and I decide to show him some of my favorite trees on the lot. Whatever tip money he wants to spend today, I'll make sure he gets the best. I begin walking toward a balsam fir I've had my eye on, but he starts heading toward the parking area.

I stop. "Where are you going?"

He turns around. "I don't have any money for a tree right now," he says. His smile is warm but mischievous. "I got what I came for."

CHAPTER NINE

Things slow down Sunday evening, so I retreat to the trailer to chat with Rachel and Elizabeth. I open my laptop and slide apart the curtains by the table in case I'm needed outside. As my friends' faces appear onscreen, my heart aches from being so far away. Within minutes, though, I'm laughing as Rachel describes how her Spanish teacher tried to get the class to make empanadas.

"They were like burnt hockey pucks," she says. "I'm not lying! After class, we literally played hockey in the hallways."

"I miss you guys so much," I say. I reach out to touch their faces on the screen and they touch the screen right back.

"How are things?" Elizabeth asks. "Not to be pushy, but any news about next year?"

"Well, I did bring it up," I say. "My parents really want to make it work here, but so far I don't know if things are heading that way. I'm sure that makes you all a little happy, but—"

"No," Elizabeth says. "No matter what happens, it's going to be bittersweet."

"We would never want the tree lot to end," Rachel says, "but of course we'd love you to be here with us."

I look out the window. Three customers are all I can see moving in the trees. "It doesn't feel like we've been as busy as last year," I tell them. "My parents analyze our sales every night, but I'm too afraid to ask."

"Then don't," Elizabeth says. "Whatever happens will happen."

She's right, but every time I leave to do homework or even take a break, I wonder if I could be doing more. Losing this place would be so hard, especially for Dad.

Rachel leans in. "Okay, is it my turn? You will not believe the ridiculousness I'm dealing with for the winter formal. I'm working with a bunch of amateurs!" She launches into a story about sending two freshmen to a craft store for supplies to make snowflakes. They came back with glitter.

"That's it?" I ask.

"Glitter! Didn't they realize we'd need something to put the glitter *on*? We're not throwing it in the air!"

I imagine being at a formal like that; classmates in gowns and tuxes flinging up handfuls of glitter as they dance. The glitter cascades down, lit by the swirling lights. Rachel and Elizabeth laugh and spin with their arms out. And I watch Caleb, his head tipped back and his eyes closed, smiling.

"So . . . I met someone," I say. "Sort of."

There's a pause that feels like forever.

"As in, a boy?" Rachel asks.

"Right now we're just friends," I say. "I think."

"Look at you blush!" Elizabeth says.

I hide my face in my hands. "I don't know. Maybe it's nothing. You know, he's—"

Rachel interrupts. "No! No-no-no-no-*no*. You're not allowed to get fussy over what's wrong with him. Not when you're in full-on crush mode."

"I'm not being fussy this time. I'm not! He's this super sweet guy who gives Christmas trees to people who can't afford them."

Rachel leans back and crosses her arms. "But . . ."

"This is where she gets fussy," Elizabeth says.

I look from Rachel to Elizabeth, both in their little boxes on my screen. Both waiting for me to tell them the downside. "But . . . this super sweet guy may have gone after his sister with a knife."

Their mouths drop open.

"Or maybe he just pulled it on her," I say. "I don't know. I haven't asked him."

Rachel touches a fist to her head and then unfurls her fingers like her brain went *kaboom*. "A knife, Sierra?"

"It could be just a rumor," I say.

"That's a pretty serious rumor," Elizabeth says. "What does Heather think?"

"She's the one who told me."

85

Rachel leans close to her screen again. "You are the pickiest person I've met when it comes to guys. Why is this happening?"

"He knows I heard something," I say, "but he shuts down whenever it comes up."

"You need to ask him," Elizabeth says.

Rachel points a finger at me. "But do it in a public place."

They're right. Of course they're right. I need to know more before I let myself get any closer to him.

"And do it before you kiss him," Rachel adds.

I laugh. "We have to be alone for that to happen."

I feel my eyes go wide, remembering that we will be alone tomorrow. Sometime after Caleb gets out of school he's taking me with him to deliver a tree.

"Ask him," Rachel says. "If it's all a misunderstanding, it will be such a good story to tell when you get home."

"I am not falling for a guy so you have something to tell your theater friends," I say.

"Trust your instincts," Elizabeth says. "Maybe Heather heard the rumor wrong. Wouldn't he be in some sort of special home if he stabbed his sister?"

"I didn't say he stabbed her. I don't know what happened exactly."

"See?" Elizabeth says. "I messed up the rumor already."

"I will get a chance to ask tomorrow," I say. "We're going out to deliver a Christmas tree together."

Rachel leans back. "You live a weird life, girl."

Even though Mom and Dad are still inside the trailer finishing a late dinner, I can feel their eyes watching Caleb and me as we walk to his truck. With their eyes on us, and Caleb's hand one outstretched finger from mine, this feels like one of the longest walks of my life.

I climb into the passenger seat of his truck and he shuts my door. Behind me in the bed of the truck is another Christmas tree. It's a heavily discounted—sorry, Dad—noble fir, and we're about to drive to wherever this tree is wanted. In all my time on this lot, season after season, I've never followed a tree from the time it left our possession to its eventual home.

"I was telling my friends about this tree distribution of yours," I say. "They think it's very sweet."

He laughs as he starts up the truck. "Tree *distribution*, huh? I always thought I was delivering them."

"It means the same thing! Are you still on me about my word choice?" I don't mention that I kind of like it.

"Maybe I'll pick up some of your vocab tricks before you head home."

I reach over and nudge his shoulder. "You should be so lucky."

He smiles at me and puts the truck in gear. "I guess that'll depend on how much I get to see you."

I glance at him, and as his words register, warmth runs through me.

When we reach the main road, he asks, "Any thoughts on how often that'll be?"

I wish I could give him an answer, but before I make

projections on our time together, there are things I need to know. I just wish *he'd* bring it up, like he said he would.

"It depends," I say. "How many more trees do you think you'll give out this year?"

He looks out his window into the next lane, but his smile reflects in the side-view mirror. "It's the holidays, so my tips are decent, but I must say, even discounted trees get expensive. No offense."

"Well, I can't discount any more than I am, so maybe you'll need to lay on the charm extra thick at work."

We pull onto the highway heading north. The ragged pyramid of Cardinals Peak is silhouetted against the darkening sky.

I point toward the top of the hill. "I bet you didn't know I have six Christmas trees growing up there."

He glances at me briefly and then looks out the window to the dark and looming hill. "You have a Christmas tree farm on Cardinals Peak?"

"Not exactly a farm," I say, "but I've been planting one a year."

"Really? How did you start something like that?" he asks.

"It actually goes back to when I was five years old."

He puts on the turn signal, checks over his shoulder, and then slides us into the next lane. "Don't hold back," he says. "I want the full origin story." Headlights of passing cars light up his curious smile.

"Okay then." I hold on to the seat belt strapped across my chest. "Back home when I was five, I planted this one tree with my mom. Before that I had planted dozens of trees, but this one we kept separate. We put a fence around it and everything. Six years later, when I was eleven, we cut it down and gave it to the maternity ward of our hospital."

"Good for you," he says.

"It's nothing like what you're doing, Mr. Charity," I say. "Giving them a tree was something my parents did every Christmas to say thank you after I was born. Apparently it took a long time for me to agree to join this world."

"My mom says my sister was fussy at birth, too," Caleb says.

I laugh. "My friends would love to know you just described me that way."

He looks at me, but there is no way I'm explaining that one.

"Anyway, this one year we decided to plant a tree for them that would be specifically from me. At the time, I loved the idea. But skip ahead six years and I had taken such good care of that tree for its entire life—for almost *my* entire life—that when we cut it down I cried so hard. My mom says I knelt in front of its stump and cried for an hour."

"Aw!" Caleb says.

"If you like sentimental, wait until I tell you that the tree cried, too. Sort of," I say. "When a tree grows it sucks up water through its roots, right? When it's cut down, sometimes the roots keep pushing water up to the stump in little droplets of sap."

"Like tears?" he says. "That's heartbreaking!"

"I know!"

Headlights shining into the cab reveal a smirk on his face. "But you have to admit, it's also kind of sappy."

I roll my eyes. "I have heard every sap joke you could think of, mister."

He signals again and we drive to the next off-ramp. It's a tight curve and I hold on to the door.

"That's why we cut an inch from the bottom of the trees before we let people take them off the lot," I say. "It gets you restarted with a clean cut that will keep pulling up water. It can't drink when it's sealed with sap."

"Does that really . . . ?" He stops himself. "Oh, I know, that's a smart thing to do."

"Anyway," I say. "After we brought my tree to the hospital, Dad gave me that inch-thick slice he'd cut from the base. I took it to my room and painted a Christmas tree on one side of it, and I still have it propped on my dresser at home."

"I love that," Caleb says. "I don't know if I've ever kept anything that symbolic. But how does that lead to your little farm on the mountain?"

"So the next day, we were getting ready to drive down here," I say. "Actually, we'd already pulled away from the house and I started crying again. I realized that I should have planted a tree to replace the one we cut down. We had to get going, though, so I made my mom pull up to our greenhouse and I grabbed a baby tree in a pot and buckled it into the backseat."

"And then you planted it here," he says.

"After that, I brought a tree down with me every season. My plan has always been to cut that first one down next year and give it to Heather's family. They always get one from us, but that one will be special," I say.

"That is a great story," he says.

"Thanks." I look out my window as we drive past a couple of blocks of two-story hotels. Then I close my eyes, wondering if I should say this. "But what if . . . I don't know . . . what if you gave that tree to someone who needed it?"

We drive another block in silence. Finally, I look over at him expecting to see a sincere smile on his face. I just offered to let him give away the first tree I planted in California. Instead, he stares at the road, lost in thought.

"I thought you would like that," I say.

He blinks and then looks at me. A cautious smile passes his lips. "Thanks."

Really? I want to say. *Because you don't look very happy about it.*

He rolls down his window a crack and the air plays with his hair. "I'm sorry," he says. "I was picturing your tree in a stranger's house. You already had plans for it. They were good plans. Don't change that because of me."

"Well, maybe that's what I want."

Caleb pulls the truck into the parking lot of a four-story apartment complex. He finds an open spot close to the building, steers into it, and parks. "How about this: I'll keep an eye out all year for the perfect family. When you come back, we can bring it to their place together."

I try to conceal any uncertainty about next year. "And what if I don't want to hang out with you next year?"

His face shutters, and I immediately regret it. I had hoped for a sarcastic comeback, but instead I scramble for a way to recover. "I mean, what if you don't have any teeth next year? You do have that addiction to candy canes and hot chocolate . . ."

He smiles and opens his door. "Tell you what: I'll brush my teeth extra well all year long." The heaviness falls away.

I climb out of the truck smiling and walk toward the back. Most of the apartment windows are dark, but a few of them have Christmas lights around them. Caleb meets me at the tailgate, which he lowers, hiding the Sagebrush Junior High bumper sticker. He begins to pull out the tree by the trunk, and I reach into the branches to help.

"Now that I'm improving your hygiene *and* your vocabulary," I say, "is there anything else you need help with?"

He gives me a dimpled grin and nods toward the apartments. "Just start walking. You'd have to clear your entire schedule to help me out."

I lead the way, and we carry the tree toward the building's entrance. I close my eyes and laugh, not believing what I almost blurted out. I look back over my shoulder and somehow suppress telling him, "Consider it cleared."

CHAPTER TEN

The elevator is almost too small for us to prop the tree straight up. Caleb kicks the button for the third floor and soon we're rising. When the door opens again, I squeeze out first, Caleb tips the tree forward, and I grab it. We carry it to the end of the hallway, where he knocks on the last door with his knee. An angel cut from construction paper, probably by a young child, is thumbtacked to the peephole. The angel holds a banner that reads *Feliz Navidad.*

A heavyset gray-haired woman in a floral-print dress opens the door. She steps back in happy surprise. "Caleb!"

Still holding the trunk of the tree, he says, "Merry Christmas, Mrs. Trujillo."

"Luis didn't tell me you were coming. And with a tree!"

"He wanted it to be a surprise," Caleb says. "Mrs. Trujillo, I'd like you to meet my friend Sierra."

Mrs. Trujillo looks ready to wrap me in a hug but sees that my hands are fairly occupied. "It is so nice to meet you," she says. While we lug the tree inside, I catch her wink at Caleb while nodding at me, but I pretend not to notice.

"The food bank told me you would love a tree," Caleb says, "so I'm glad I could bring it over."

The woman blushes and pats his arm a bunch of times. "Oh, sweet boy. Such a big heart!" She shuffles in her slippers across the dual living room and dining room. She leans down, her belly straining the floral pattern on her dress, and pulls a tree stand from beneath the couch. "We haven't even got up the fake tree yet, Luis is so busy with school. And now you brought me a real tree!"

Caleb and I hold the tree between us while she kicks aside magazines and places the stand in the corner. We listen to her go on about how much she loves the smell.

She looks at Caleb, touches her heart, and then claps one time. "Thank you, Caleb. Thank you, thank you, thank you."

A voice calls from the other side of the room, "I think he heard you, Mama."

Caleb looks at a guy about our age who must be Luis walking out of a narrow hallway. "Hey, man."

"Luis! Look what Caleb brought to us."

Luis looks at the tree with an uneasy smile. "Thanks for bringing it over."

Mrs. Trujillo touches my arm. "Do you go to school with the boys?"

"I live up in Oregon, actually," I say.

"Her parents own a tree lot in town," Caleb says. "That's where this one's from."

"It is?" She looks at me. "Are you teaching Caleb to be your delivery boy?"

Luis laughs, but Mrs. Trujillo looks confused.

"No," Caleb says. He looks at me. "Not really. We . . ."

I stare right back. "Go on." I would love to hear him explain what we are.

He smirks. "We've become good friends the past few days."

Mrs. Trujillo raises both of her hands. "I understand. I ask too much questions. Caleb, will you bring some *turrón* to your mother and father for me?"

"Absolutely!" Caleb says. He looks at her like she offered him a glass of water in the middle of the desert. "Sierra, you have got to try this stuff."

Mrs. Trujillo claps her hands. "Yes! You must take some for your family, too. I made so much. Luis and I are going to take some to the neighbors later."

She orders Luis to bring her some napkins and then she hands us each a piece of what looks like peanut brittle but with almonds. I break off a piece and pop it in my mouth—so delicious! Caleb's already devoured half of his piece.

Mrs. Trujillo beams. She puts a few more pieces into sandwich bags for us to take home. Walking to the front door, we both thank her again for the *turrón*. She hugs Caleb for a long time after he opens the door, expressing gratitude again for the tree.

Waiting for the elevator door to open, *turrón* baggies in hand, I ask, "So, Luis is a friend?"

"I was hoping it wouldn't get awkward," he says, nodding. The elevator door opens, we enter, and he presses the bottom button. "The food bank keeps a list of items where families can mark down things they need. I had them occasionally ask some families if they could use a tree, and that's where I get the addresses. When I saw theirs pop up, I asked Luis if it was okay, but . . ."

"He didn't seem that thrilled," I say. "Do you think he was embarrassed?"

"He'll get over it," Caleb says. "He knew his mom wanted one. And I guarantee you, she is the nicest woman."

The elevator door opens at the ground floor and Caleb motions for me to walk out first.

"She's so grateful for everything," Caleb says. "She doesn't judge anyone. Someone like her deserves to get what she wants once in a while."

Back in the truck, we drive to the highway and start heading to the lot.

"So why do you do this?" I ask, deciding the trees are a safe way to inch us into more personal areas.

He drives about half a block with no response. Finally, he says, "I guess you did tell me about your trees on the hill . . ."

"Fair is fair," I tell him.

"Why I do it is similar to why I know Luis will get over it," he says. "He knows it's sincere. For a while after my parents divorced, we were in the same boat as the Trujillos. My mom barely made enough to buy us small gifts, let alone a tree."

I add that to a small but growing list of things I know about Caleb. "How are things now?" I ask.

"They're better. She's the head of her department now, and we're back to having trees. That first one I bought at the lot was for us." He looks at me briefly and smiles. "She still won't get excessive with decorating, but she knows the trees meant a lot to us growing up."

I picture all those one-dollar bills from his first visit. "But you paid for the tree."

"Not all of it." He laughs. "I just made sure we got a bigger one."

I want to ask about his sister. But the profile of his face as he looks through the windshield appears so calm. Heather's right, whatever's going on here doesn't have to last past Christmas. If I enjoy being around him, why mess that up? Asking will only make him shut down again.

Or maybe, to be honest, I don't want to know the answer.

"I'm glad we got to do this tonight," I say. "Thank you."

He grins and then puts on a signal to exit the highway.

Caleb told me he would stop by the lot again later in the week. When his truck finally pulls up, I stay in the Bigtop rather than walk out to greet him. I don't need him to know how eagerly I've anticipated this. I kind of hope that's why he didn't come by the very next day; he was hiding the same anticipation.

When more than enough time goes by for him to find me, I peek outside. Andrew is saying something to him, stressing points by jabbing a finger toward the ground. Caleb's eyes fix in a tense stare somewhere beyond Andrew, his hands pressed deep in his jacket pockets. When Andrew points a sharp finger at our trailer—where Dad is inside on the phone with Uncle Bruce—Caleb closes his eyes and his arms go slack. Andrew soon walks off into the trees and I half expect him to shove one out of his way.

I quickly retreat behind the counter. Several seconds later, Caleb comes into the Bigtop. He doesn't know I saw the exchange with Andrew, and he acts like everything's normal.

"I'm heading to work," he says, and now I know he can fake that dimpled smile. "But I couldn't drive by without saying hi."

We're not alone for more than a minute before Dad sets his work gloves on the counter and then twists off the lid of his thermos. He goes to refill his coffee. Without looking up, he asks, "You here to pick up another tree?"

"No, sir," Caleb says. "Not right now. I just stopped by to say hi to Sierra."

When the thermos is full, Dad turns toward Caleb. Holding the thermos steady, he slowly tightens the lid. "As long as you keep it short. She's got a lot of work here to do, and then schoolwork."

Dad pats Caleb on the shoulder as he walks past him and I want to die of humiliation. We talk for a couple more minutes in the Bigtop and then I walk Caleb to his truck. He opens the driver's side door, but before he gets in he nods toward the parade poster I hung when I first met him.

"That's tomorrow night," he says. "I'll be down there with some friends. You should show up."

Show up? I want to tease him for not being brave enough to ask me to meet him there.

"I'll think about it," I say.

After he drives away I head back to the Bigtop, looking at the ground and smiling.

Before I get to the counter, Dad walks in front of me.

"Sierra . . ." He knows I don't want to hear what he's going to say next, but he has to say it anyway. "I'm sure he's a nice kid, but please be wary about starting something now. You're busy, and then we're leaving and—"

"I'm not starting anything," I say. "I made a friend, Dad. Stop being weird."

He laughs and then sips his coffee. "Why can't you go back to playing princess?"

"I *never* played princess."

"Are you kidding?" he says. "Whenever Heather's mom took the two of you to the parade, you wore your fanciest dress, pretending to be the Winter Queen."

"Exactly!" I say. "Queen, not princess. You raised me better than that."

Dad bows low, as he should in the presence of royalty. Then he walks toward the trailer and I return to the Bigtop. Inside, leaning against the counter, is Andrew.

I walk behind the counter and push Dad's work gloves aside. "What were you and Caleb talking about out there?"

"I notice he's been coming around a lot," Andrew says.

I cross my arms. "So?"

Andrew shakes his head. "You think he's a great guy because he buys people trees. But you don't know him."

I want to argue that *he* doesn't know anything about Caleb, but the truth is, he probably knows more than me. Am I dumb for not confronting Caleb about the rumor yet?

"If your dad doesn't want any of his workers asking you out," Andrew says, "there is no way he'd approve of Caleb."

"Stop!" I say. "This has nothing to do with you."

He looks down. "Last year I was dumb. I left that stupid note on your window when I should have asked you to your face."

"Andrew," I say softly, "it's not my dad or Caleb or anyone else. Let's not make working together any more awkward, okay?"

He looks at me and his expression goes hard. "Don't do this with Caleb. You're ridiculous to even think you can be friends with him. He is not who you think he is. Don't be—"

"Say it!" My eyes narrow. If he calls me stupid, Dad will fire him in a second.

Andrew cuts his words short and leaves abruptly.

CHAPTER ELEVEN

The evening of the parade, I head downtown with Heather and Devon. Heather's mom is on the parade committee and begged us to arrive early. The moment we show up at the blue canopy marked *Registration,* she hands each of us a bag of participant ribbons and a clipboard to check off entries. Most of the groups are already accounted for, but every year some new organizations line up and forget to check in. She tells us it's our job to track them down.

Devon looks at Heather. "Seriously? We have to do this?"

"Yes, Devon. It's one of the perks of being my boyfriend. If you don't like it . . ." She motions toward the people walking by.

Undeterred by the challenge in her words, Devon drops a kiss on her cheek. "Totally worth it." When he pulls away, he looks at me with a subtle smirk. Yes, he is aware that he infuriates her at times.

"Before we find anyone," Heather says, "let's grab some coffee. It's getting cold out."

We weave our way through a boisterous Boy Scout troop and then down a block and a half to a café off the parade route. Heather sends Devon in and waits outside with me.

"You need to tell him," I say. "It's not doing either of you any good to prolong this."

She tilts her head back and sighs. "I know. But he needs better grades this semester. I don't want to be the one to distract him from that."

"Heather . . ."

"I'm the worst. I know! I know." She looks me in the eyes but then sees something in the distance behind me. "Speaking of conversations that need to happen, I think that's Caleb."

I spin around. Across the street, Caleb sits on the back of a bus bench with two other guys. One of them looks like Luis. I decide to wait for Devon to come out with our coffees while I gather up the courage to walk over.

A bus rumbles up to the bench and I worry that I missed my chance. When the bus pulls away, Caleb and his friends remain sitting there, talking and laughing. Caleb rubs his hands briskly together and then shoves them in his coat pockets. Devon comes out and offers me one of the coffees, but I shake my head.

"I'm changing my order," I tell them. "Will you two check people in without me? I can meet up with you later."

"Of course," Heather says. Devon sighs, obviously annoyed that I get to cut out of parade work while he has to stay. Before he can complain, though, Heather looks at him and says, "Because! That's why."

When I come out of the café, I carry a hot drink in each hand. I cross the street slowly so nothing sloshes out of the lids. Before I reach Caleb, several yards beyond them, I notice a tall guy in a white marching band uniform climb out of a car. Sliding out next is a slightly older girl in a cheer uniform with the Bulldogs mascot on the chest.

Another band member carrying a flute jogs up to them. "Jeremiah!"

Caleb shifts his attention from his friends on the bench to the band members. Jeremiah opens the trunk of the car and removes a snare drum with a long strap. He shuts the trunk, loops the strap over one arm, and shoves two drumsticks in his back pocket.

I slow down as I get close to the bench. Caleb hasn't turned my way yet, still focused on the band members and the cheerleader. The car rolls forward and I see the woman driving the car lean over and look up at Caleb. He gives her a hesitant smile and then looks down.

The car drives away and I can hear the flutist talk about a girl he's meeting after the parade. When they pass the bench, Jeremiah looks over at Caleb. It's hard to tell for sure, but I see a hint of sadness in both of them.

The cheerleader walks up and grabs Jeremiah's elbow, moving them on. When Caleb's gaze follows them, he catches sight of me.

"You made it," he says.

I offer one of the drinks. "You looked cold."

He takes a sip and then covers his mouth as he almost laughs. After he swallows, he says, "Peppermint mocha. Of course it is."

"And not the cheap kind, either," I say.

Luis and the other guy lean forward to look at something down the street beyond me. At the intersection is a parked pink-and-white stretch convertible. The back door is being held open, and a high school girl in a blue shimmering gown and light blue sash is helped into the backseat.

"Is that Christy Wang?" I ask. Back when I went to elementary school here a few weeks each year, Christy was the one person who never let me feel welcome. I wasn't a real Californian, she said. She must have turned her personality around enough to win Winter Queen. Or maybe it has more to do with how incredible she looks in that dress.

"It's a beautiful day for a parade, folks," Luis says in a weird announcer voice. "Just beautiful! And this year's Winter Queen is certainly a hottie. I'm guessing Santa placed her at the tippy top of his very, *very* Nice List."

The guy sitting next to Luis cracks up.

Caleb jokingly shoves them into each other. "Dude. Show some respect. She's our Queen."

"What in the world are you guys doing?" I ask.

The guy I don't know says, "It's parade commentary. Every year there's a weird lack of TV coverage, so we're doing this town a favor. I'm Brent, by the way."

I hold out my free hand. "Sierra."

Caleb looks at me, embarrassed. "It's an annual tradition."

Brent points a finger at me. "You're the Christmas tree girl. I've definitely heard about you."

Caleb takes a big swig and shrugs, feigning innocence.

"Nice to see you again, Luis," I say.

"You too," he says. His voice is soft, perhaps laced with self-consciousness. He perks up after a man with an untied shoe walks by. "Let's hear it for the Trendsetters Club, everyone. Start by tying one shoelace tight and then let the other hang loose. If you're cool, it's bound to catch on. This one? It ain't catching on."

"Don't trip, trendsetter!" Brent says. The man looks back, and Brent smiles and waves at him.

No one says anything for several seconds as they all sit and watch people pass by. Caleb takes another sip and I slowly step back.

"Where are you going?" he says. "Stay."

"It's okay. I don't want to interrupt your announcing job."

Caleb looks at his friends. Some silent guy communication happens and then he turns to me. "Nope. We're good."

Brent shoos us away with his hands. "You children run along and have fun."

Caleb fist-bumps his friends and then steers me toward the parade route. "Thanks again for the drink."

We walk past a few stores open late for the parade crowd. I turn toward him, hoping a lighthearted conversation will begin to flow. He looks at me and we smile at each other, but then we both face forward again. I feel so off my game with Caleb, so unsure and awkward.

Finally, I ask the one thing truly on my mind: "Who was that guy back there?"

"Brent?"

"The drummer in the marching band."

Caleb takes a sip and we walk a few more steps in silence. "Jeremiah. He's an old friend."

"And he'd rather march in a parade than do commentary with all of you?" I ask. "Shocking."

He smiles. "No, probably not. But he wouldn't be hanging out with us even if he could."

After a long hesitation, I ask, "Is there a story there?"

His answer is immediate. "It's a long story, Sierra."

I'm obviously prying, but then why would I consider even a friendship with him if I can't ask a simple question? It's not like the question came out of nowhere. It was regarding something that happened right in front of me. If something that small shuts him down, I don't know if I want to stick around. I've walked away for much less than this.

"You can go back to your friends if you want," I say. "I need to help Heather anyway."

"I'd rather come with you," he says.

I stop. "Caleb, I think you should be with your friends tonight."

He closes his eyes and scrubs a hand through his hair. "Let me try again."

I look at him, waiting.

"Jeremiah was my best friend. Stuff happened, which I guess you've heard some of, and his parents didn't want him hanging around me anymore. His sister is sort of the hall monitor—a mini version of his mom—and she somehow manages to always be around."

I replay the way Jeremiah's mom looked at Caleb as she drove by and his sister marched him down the sidewalk. I want to ask for more details, but he needs to *want* to tell me. The only way we can get closer is if he's the one asking me in.

"If you need to know what happened, I'll tell you," Caleb says, "but not now."

"Then soon," I say.

"Just not here. It's a Christmas parade! And we've got peppermint mochas." He looks at something behind me and smirks. "Anyway, you'd probably miss some of what I said because of the band."

As if on cue, the marching band breaks into a loud, percussive rendition of "Little Drummer Boy."

I shout over them to be heard. "Point taken!"

We find Heather and Devon standing a block from where the parade begins. Devon clutches the clipboard to his chest, almost like a security blanket, while Heather glares at him.

"What's up?" I ask.

"The Winter Queen asked for his number!" Heather blurts. "And I was standing right there!"

A tiny smile passes over Devon's lips, and I almost smile back. Christy Wang has not changed at all. It also makes me wonder whether all of Heather's talk about breaking up was just that . . . talk. She has to feel something for him, even if it only comes out as jealousy.

Caleb and I follow them to a small gap between families sitting on the curb to watch the parade. Heather sits down first and I squish up close beside her. Devon remains standing and Caleb gives him a fist bump before sitting next to me.

"She really asked for his number?" I say.

"Yes!" Heather hisses. "And I was standing right there!"

Devon leans forward. "I didn't give it to her, though. I told her I already had a girl."

"*Had* is almost right," Heather says.

"She *is* a good-looking Winter Queen," Caleb adds.

I hear the teasing in his voice, but I elbow him anyway. "Not cool."

He smiles and bats his eyes like Mr. Innocent. Before Heather can say anything more, or Devon can dig himself a deeper hole, the Bulldogs marching band rounds the corner, led by the cheerleaders. The crowd cheers along to their instrumental "Jingle Bell Rock."

I watch Jeremiah pass, drumsticks pattering away. We all clap along, but I slowly stop and study Caleb. After everyone else has turned to see the next group in the parade, Caleb's eyes are still on the band. The drums are distant now but he keeps the rhythm, tapping his fingers against his knees.

🌲

Caleb shuts the tailgate behind another tree in the back of his truck. "Are you sure you have time for this?" he asks.

Actually, I do not have time for this. The lot gets slammed after the parade every year, but we came straight back and I asked Mom if I could go on this one run with Caleb. She gave me thirty minutes.

"It's not a problem at all," I say. Two more cars pull up to our lot and he gives me a skeptical look. "Okay, maybe it's not the most convenient time, but I want to do this."

He dimple-grins and walks around to his door. "Good."

We pull up to a small, dark house only a few minutes away and both get out. He takes the middle of the tree and I grab the trunk. We walk up a few concrete steps to the front door and adjust our grips. At the sound of Caleb ringing the doorbell I can feel my heart start to race. I've always enjoyed selling trees, but surprising people with them is a whole new level of excitement.

The door opens fast. An irritated man glares from Caleb to the tree. An exhausted-looking woman beside him gives the same look to me.

"The food bank said you were coming earlier," he snaps. "We missed the parade waiting for you!"

Caleb drops his gaze momentarily. "I am so sorry. I told them we'd be here after the parade."

Through the doorway, I see a playpen in the living room with a diapered baby asleep inside of it.

"That's not what they told us. So were they lying?" the woman says. She pulls the door open wider and nods into the house. "Just put it in the stand."

Caleb and I carry in the tree, which now feels ten times heavier, and get it set up in a dark corner while they watch. After adjusting it a few times to make it as straight as possible, we stand back and look it over with the man. When he doesn't object, Caleb motions for me to follow him back to the door.

"I do hope you have a merry Christmas," Caleb says.

"It's not off to a great start," the woman mutters. "We missed the parade for this."

I begin to twist around. "We heard you the—"

Caleb grabs my hand and pulls me toward the door. "Again, we're very sorry."

I follow him out the door, shaking my head. When we get back in the truck, I unload. "They didn't even say thank you. Not once!"

Caleb starts the engine. "They missed the parade. They were frustrated."

I blink. "Are you serious? You brought them a free tree!"

Caleb throws the truck into reverse and eases into the street. "I'm not doing this to earn a gold star. They had a little baby and they were probably tired. Missing the parade—misunderstanding or not—would be frustrating."

"But you're doing this with your own money on your own time . . ."

He looks at me and smiles. "So you would only do this if people tell you how awesome you are for it?"

I want to scream and laugh about how ridiculous those people were. About how ridiculous Caleb is being right now! Instead, I'm left speechless and he knows it. He laughs and then looks over his shoulder to change lanes.

I like Caleb. I like him even more every time I see him. And this can only lead to disaster. I'm leaving at the end of the month, he's staying, and the weight of everything not said between us is growing too heavy to carry much longer.

Back at the lot, Caleb puts the truck in park but keeps the engine running. "Just so you know, I am very aware of how mean they were about getting a free tree. I have to believe, though, that everyone is allowed a bad day."

The lights surrounding the lot bring shadows into Caleb's truck. He looks at me, his features half hidden, but his eyes catch the light and beg to be understood.

"I agree," I say.

CHAPTER TWELVE

It's the busiest day at the lot so far. I barely have time to go to the bathroom, let alone eat lunch. So I pick at a bowl of mac and cheese at the counter in the rare moments between ringing up customers. Monsieur Cappeau sent an email this morning asking me to call him over the next day or so *pour pratiquer*, but that's way down on my need-to-do list.

Today's tree delivery came early again, not only before we opened but before any of the workers even arrived. Dad called a few of the more dependable ballplayers to come in early, so at least there were a handful of us to tiredly unload the shipment.

As exhausted as I am from unloading so many trees before breakfast, I'm grateful for the extra business. It feels like things may be picking up, and keeping the lot open another year could be a possibility.

I stand beside Mom at the register and point toward Mr. and Mrs. Ramsay outside. I attempt some tree lot commentary, like Caleb and his friends at the parade.

"Folks, it looks like the Ramsays are arguing over whether or not to pay extra for this stunning white pine," I say.

Mom looks at me as if questioning my sanity, but I continue.

"We've seen this before," I say, "and I don't think I'm spoiling it to tell you Mrs. Ramsay *will* get her way. She's never been a fan of the blue spruce, no matter what Mr. Ramsay says."

Mom laughs, motioning for me to keep my voice down.

"A decision looks imminent!" I say.

Now we're both glued to the scene playing out within our trees.

"Mrs. Ramsay is flapping her arms," I say, "calling for her husband to just make up his mind if he wants to bring home anything at all. Mr. Ramsay compares the needles on both trees. What's it going to be, folks? What's it going to be? And . . . it's . . . the . . . white pine!"

Mom and I throw our hands in the air and then I give her a high five.

"Mrs. Ramsay wins again," I say.

The couple enters the Bigtop and Mom, biting her cheeks, ducks out. When Mr. Ramsay sets the final twenty-dollar bill on the counter, Mrs. Ramsay and I exchange knowing smiles. I hate to see anyone leave even slightly discouraged, so I tell Mr. Ramsay they made a great choice. White pines hold their needles better than some trees. They won't need to vacuum them up before their grandkids arrive.

Before he can put away his wallet, Mrs. Ramsay takes it from him and slides me a ten-dollar tip for my help. They both leave happy, although she good-naturedly swats him and tells him he's too cheap for his own good.

I stare at the ten-dollar bill, a hazy idea taking shape. I rarely receive tips since most people tip the guys who load their trees.

I send a text to Heather: **Can we do some cookie making at your house tonight?** Our trailer is a good home away from home, but it's not built for a baking frenzy.

Heather texts back right away: **Of course!**

I immediately text Caleb: **If you do a delivery tomorrow, I want to go. I'll even have something to contribute besides my beguiling personality. I bet you never used that in a sentence!**

A few minutes later, Caleb responds: **I have not. And yes you may.**

I tuck my phone away, smiling to myself. For the rest of the afternoon and evening the anticipation of spending more time with Caleb keeps me going. But as I count out the register at closing, I'm aware that this time needs to be about more than trees and cookies. If he makes me feel this happy now, and I can easily see things growing more intense, I need to know what happened with his sister. He did admit something happened, but knowing all that I do about him and all that I've seen, I can't imagine it's as bad as what some people believe.

At least, I hope it's not.

Time drags at half-speed the next day. Heather and I were up late talking and baking Christmas cookies at her house. Devon stopped by in time to add frosting and sprinkles and help us sample about a dozen of them. With firsthand experience now, I agree that his stories are mind-numbing. His skills at cookie design *almost* made up for it, though.

I finish showing a customer how to price our trees based on the colored ribbons tied to them. Once he gets it and moves on, I hold on to one of the trees and close my heavy eyes for a moment. Upon opening them, I see Caleb's truck pull in and feel suddenly fully awake.

Dad notices the truck, too. When I head to the Bigtop, he meets me at the register, a few tree needles stuck to his hair.

"Still spending time with this boy?" he asks. The tone is embarrassingly obvious.

I flick a few needles from his shoulder. "The boy's name is Caleb," I say, "and he doesn't work here, so you can't scare him out of talking to me. Plus, you have to admit, he is our best customer."

"Sierra . . ." He doesn't finish, but I want him to know that I'm not blind to our circumstance.

"We're only here a few more weeks. I know. You don't need to say it."

"I just don't want you getting your hopes up," he says. "Or his, for that matter. Remember, we don't even know if we're coming back next year."

I swallow past the lump in my throat. "Maybe it doesn't make sense," I say. "And I'm fully aware that I'm not usually like this, but . . . I like him."

The way he winces, anyone watching would think I told him I was pregnant. Dad shakes his head. "Sierra, be—"

"Careful? Is that the cliché you're looking for?"

He looks away. The unspoken irony is that he and Mom met this exact way. On *this* lot.

I brush another needle from his hair and kiss him on the cheek. "I hope you think I usually am."

Caleb approaches the counter and sets down a tag from his next tree. "Tonight's family is getting a beauty," he says. "I noticed it the last time I was here."

Dad smiles at him and politely claps him on the shoulder and then walks away without muttering a word.

"That means you're winning him over," I explain. I grab a sleigh-shaped cookie tin from below the register and Caleb raises his eyebrows. "Stop salivating. These are staying wherever we take the tree."

"Wait, you made those for them?" I swear, it's like his smile lights up the entire Bigtop.

After we deliver the tree and cookies to tonight's family, Caleb asks if I would like to taste the best pancake in town. I agree, and he drives us to a twenty-four-hour diner that was probably last remodeled in the mid-1970s. A long stretch of windows lit by orange-hued lights frame a dozen booths. There are only two people seated inside, at opposite ends of the diner.

"Do we need to get tetanus shots to eat here?" I ask.

"This is the only place in town you can get a pancake as big as your head," he says. "And do not tell me that hasn't been a dream of yours."

Inside the diner, a handwritten sign duct-taped to the register says *Please seat yourself.* I follow Caleb to a window booth, walking beneath red Christmas ornaments hung by fishing line to the ceiling tiles. We slide into a booth whose green vinyl covering has seen better days, but more than likely not in this century. After we each order the "world famous" pancake I fold my hands on the table and look at him. He thumbs the top of a large syrup pourer beside the napkins, sliding the lid open and shut.

"There's no marching band," I prompt. "If we talk, I should be able to hear you just fine."

He stops playing with the syrup and leans back against the booth. "You really want to hear this?"

I honestly don't know. He knows I've heard the rumors. Maybe I haven't heard the truth. If the truth is better, he should jump at the chance to tell me.

He picks at the cuticle on his thumb.

"You can start by explaining why you haven't used your new comb," I say. The joke falls flat, but I hope he knows I'm trying.

"I used it this morning," he says. He scrubs his fingers through his hair. "Maybe the one you got was defective."

"I doubt it," I say.

He takes a sip of water. After several more moments of silence, he asks, "Can we start by you telling me what you've heard?"

I bite my lower lip, considering how to say this. "Exact words?" I say. "Well, I heard you attacked your sister with a knife."

He closes his eyes. His body, almost undetectably, rocks back and forth. "What else?"

"That she doesn't live here anymore." It feels wrong that I even notice the butter knife on the napkin beside his hands.

"She lives in Nevada," he says, "with our dad. She's a freshman this year."

He looks toward the kitchen, maybe hoping the waitress will interrupt our conversation. Or maybe he wants to get through it without interruption.

"And you live with your mom," I say.

"Yes," he says. "Obviously that's not how things started."

The waitress sets down two empty mugs and then fills them both with coffee. We each grab creamers and packets of sugar.

He's still stirring his drink when he continues. "When my parents split, my mom took it really hard. She lost so much weight and cried a lot, which is normal, I guess. Abby and I both stayed with her while they figured things out."

He takes a sip of his drink. I pick up mine and blow away the steam.

"Abby and I were given our own lawyer, which happens

in some cases." He takes another sip and then holds his mug in both hands, staring into it. "That's when it all started. I was the one who said we should stay with our mom. I convinced Abby it's what we needed to do. I told her she needed us and that Dad would be fine."

I take a sip of my coffee while he still stares into his.

"But he wasn't fine," Caleb says. "I think I knew that for a while but I kept hoping he would pull it together. I think if I actually saw him every day, looking as hurt and broken down as my mom, I might have chosen him."

"Why do you think he wasn't fine?" I ask.

The waitress sets down our plates. The pancakes really are the size of our heads, but it does nothing to bring about the easy conversation Caleb probably hoped for when he chose this place. Still, they offer a distraction for both of us as the talk continues. I pour syrup over mine and, with a butter knife and fork, start cutting up half of it.

"Before they split, our whole family used to go nuts this time of year," he says. "We went hardcore, from decorating to all these things we did with our church. Sometimes even Pastor Tom would go caroling with us. But when Dad moved to Nevada, I found out everything did stop for him. His house was this dark and depressing place to visit. Not only were there no Christmas lights, half the regular lights in his house were burned out. He didn't even unpack most of his boxes after being there for months."

He takes a couple of bites of his pancake, looking down at his plate the whole time. I consider telling him he doesn't need to tell me more. Whatever happened, I like the Caleb sitting in front of me now.

"After our first visit to his place, Abby bugged me about him all the time. She was so mad at me for how he was dealing with things, for making us choose Mom. And she wouldn't let up about it. She'd say, 'Look what you did to him.'"

I want to tell Caleb his dad isn't his responsibility, but he must know that. I'm sure his mom told him that a thousand times. At least, I hope she has. "How old were you?" I ask.

"I was in eighth grade. Abby was in sixth."

"I can remember sixth grade," I say. "She was probably trying to figure how everything fit together in this new life you all had."

"But she blamed me for how they *weren't* fitting together. And I blamed me, because some of it was true. But I was in eighth grade. How could I know what was best for everyone?"

"Maybe there was no best," I say.

For the first time in minutes, Caleb looks up. He attempts a smile, and while it barely registers, I think he now believes that I do want to understand.

He takes a sip of his coffee, leaning forward more than lifting his hands. This is the most fragile I've seen him. "Jeremiah had been my friend for years—my best friend—and he knew how much Abby was on me about this. He called her the Wicked Witch of the West."

"That's a good friend," I say. I cut up more of my pancake.

"He'd say it in front of her, too, which of course made her even madder." He laughs a little, but when he stops, he looks out the window. His reflection against the dark glass feels cold. "One day, I snapped. I couldn't take the accusations anymore. I just snapped."

With my fork, I lift a piece of pancake dripping with syrup, but I don't bring it to my mouth. "What does that mean?"

He looks at me. His entire body echoes hurt and grief more than any remaining anger. "I couldn't listen to it anymore. I don't know how else to describe it. One day she screamed at me, the same thing she always screamed: that I'd ruined our dad's life, and hers, and Mom's. And some switch in me . . . flipped." His voice quivers. "I ran to the kitchen and grabbed a knife."

My fork remains frozen over my plate, my eyes locked with his.

"When she heard this, she ran to her room so fast," he says. "And I ran after her."

He holds on to his mug with one hand. With his other hand, he numbly folds his napkin until it conceals the butter knife. I can't tell if he's aware he did this. If he is, I don't know if it was for my sake or his.

"She got to her room and slammed the door and . . ." He leans back, closes his eyes, and puts his hands in his lap. The napkin rolls open. "I stabbed her door with the knife over and over. I didn't want to hurt her. I would *never* hurt her. But I could not stop stabbing the door. I heard her screaming and crying to our mom on the phone. Finally, I dropped the knife and just slumped onto the floor."

It comes out as a whisper, or it could be all in my head: "Oh my God."

He looks up at me. His eyes *beg* for understanding now.

"So you did it," I say.

"Sierra, I swear to you, I've never had anything like that happen to me before or since. And I promise, I would never have hurt her. I didn't even check if she locked the door, because that wasn't what it was about. I think I just needed to show how much everything was hurting me, too. I've never physically hurt anyone in my life."

"I still don't understand why," I say.

"I think I wanted to scare her," he says. "But that's all. And it did. It scared *me*. It scared my mom."

Neither of us says anything. My hands are folded tight between my knees. My entire body clenches.

"So Abby went to live with my dad, and I'm here living with the fallout and all the rumors."

All the breath has escaped me. I don't know how to reconcile the Caleb I've known and adored hanging out with and this broken person in front of me. "Do you still see her? Your sister?"

"When I visit my dad, or when she visits us here." He looks at my plate, and he must see that I haven't taken a bite in several minutes. "For almost two years, whenever she came home, we went to a family counselor. She says she understands and has forgiven me, and I think she's being honest. She's a great person. You'd love her."

Finally, I take a bite. I'm not hungry anymore, but I also don't know what to say.

"Part of me keeps hoping she'll change her mind and move back, but I could never ask for that," he says. "That has to be something *she* wants. And she likes Nevada. She has a new life there now and new friends. I suppose if there is a silver lining, I'm glad my dad has her around."

"You don't always need to find a silver lining," I say, "but I'm glad you found one."

"Still, it's had a huge impact on my mom. Because of me—without a doubt this time—one of her kids moved away," he says. "My mom's missed years of watching her daughter grow up, and that is my fault. I'll live with that forever."

The way his jaw tenses, I know he's cried over this many times. I consider everything he's told me. How hard all of this has been for his mom and sister, as well as for him. I know this should scare me a little, but somehow it doesn't, because I do believe he wouldn't hurt anyone. Everything about him makes me believe that.

"Why did your parents split?" I ask.

He shrugs. "I'm sure there's plenty I don't know, but my mom once told me she always held her breath around him, waiting for him to tell her what she was doing wrong. When they were together, I think she spent a lot of time feeling bad about herself."

"What about your sister?" I ask. "Does your dad treat her the same way?"

"No way," Caleb says, and finally he laughs. "Abby would give it right back. If he says anything about how she's dressed, she'll go on and on about double standards and he'll end up taking it all back and apologizing."

Now I laugh. "That's my kind of girl."

The waitress comes by to refill our coffee, and I see the worried creases return to Caleb's forehead.

He looks up at the waitress. "Thanks."

When she leaves, I ask, "How does Jeremiah fit into this?"

"He had the bad luck of being at my house when it happened," he says. He stares out the window again. "And he was just as freaked out as we were. He ended up going home and telling his family about it, which was fine. But that's when his mom said we couldn't be friends anymore."

"And she still won't let you see each other?"

His fingertips barely touch the lip of the table. "I'd be wrong to blame her," he says. "I know I'm not dangerous, but she's just protecting her son."

"She *thinks* she's protecting him," I say. "There's a difference."

He shifts his gaze from the window to the table between us, his eyes narrowed. "I do blame her for how she told other parents about it," he says. "She made me into this *thing* to avoid. You're only hearing about it years later because of his family. I'd be lying if I said that didn't hurt . . . a lot."

"It should never have ever gotten to me," I say.

"And she exaggerated, too," he says. "Probably to

124

make sure other parents didn't think she was overreacting. That's why I'm still a knife-wielding maniac to people like Andrew."

For the first time, I can see the anger he still holds over this.

Caleb closes his eyes and holds up a hand. "I need to take that back. I don't want you judging Jeremiah's family. I don't know for sure that she exaggerated anything. It could have changed as the story moved around."

I think about Heather's warning, and how Rachel and Elizabeth dropped their mouths in disbelief when I told them. Everyone reacted so fast. Everyone had an opinion without ever hearing from Caleb.

"Even if it was her, it doesn't matter," Caleb says. "She had a reason for saying what she did. Everyone had a reason. That doesn't change what I did to cause it."

"But it's still not fair," I say.

"For so long, whenever I walk through the halls or I walk downtown, and anyone I know looks at me but doesn't say anything—even if their look means *nothing*—I've wondered what they've heard or what they're thinking."

I shake my head. "I am so sorry, Caleb."

"The stupid thing is, I know Jeremiah and I could've stayed friends. He was there. He saw everything. I'm sure he was scared, but he knew me well enough to know I would never hurt Abby," he says. "It's just gone on too long. I was younger than she is now when it happened."

"His mom can't still be worried about her grown son

hanging out with you," I say. "No offense, but he's got a few inches on you."

He laughs once. "But she is. And so is his sister. Cassandra's almost like his shadow. Even when he has been friendly, she's right there to pull him away."

"And you're okay letting this continue?"

He looks at me, his eyes numb. "People think what they want. That's what I've had to accept," he says. "I can fight it, but that's exhausting. I can feel hurt about it, but that's torture. Or I can decide it's their loss."

No matter how he chooses to think about it, it's clear that it does still exhaust and torture him.

"It *is* their loss," I say. I reach out and place my fingers over his. "And I'm sure you would expect more impressive words from me, but you're a pretty cool guy, Caleb."

He smiles. "You're pretty cool, too, Sierra. Not that many girls would be this understanding."

I try to lighten things up. "How many girls do you need?"

"That's the other problem." His smile is lost again. "Not only would I have to explain to a girl about my past—if she hasn't already heard—I'd have to explain it to her parents. If they live here, eventually they're going to hear the rumors."

"Have you had to explain a lot?"

"No," he says, "because I haven't been with anyone long enough to find out if they're worth it."

My breath escapes me. Am *I* worth it? Is that what he's admitting?

I pull back my hands. "Is that why you're interested in me? Because I'm leaving?"

His shoulders fall and he leans back. "You want the truth?"

"I believe that's what tonight's about."

"Yes, at first, I thought maybe we could sidestep the drama and just hang out."

"But I heard the rumors," I say. "You knew that, yet you kept coming around anyway."

I can see he's holding back a smile. "Maybe it was the way you used *peruse* in a sentence." He puts his hands in the middle of the table, palms up.

"I'm sure that was it," I say. I place my hands into his. A weight has lifted for both of us tonight.

"Don't forget," he says with a childlike grin, "you also give great discounts on trees."

"Oh, *that's* why you come around," I say. "And if I decide you need to start paying full price?"

He sits back, and I know he's debating how much to keep teasing. "I guess I'd have to start paying full price."

I lift an eyebrow at him. "Then I guess it really is just me."

He runs his thumbs along my knuckles. "It's just you."

CHAPTER THIRTEEN

After I buckle in, Caleb starts the truck. We pull out of the diner's parking lot and he says, "Now it's your turn. I'd love to hear about a time *you* completely lost it."

"Me?" I say. "Oh, I'm always in control."

The way he smiles, I'm glad he knows I'm joking.

We drive onto the highway in silence. I look from the oncoming car lights to the impressive silhouette of Cardinals Peak just outside the city. I look back to him, and his profile flickers from silhouette to a happy expression, and then from silhouette to worry. Does he wonder whether I feel differently about him now?

"I gave you a lot of ammunition back there," he says.

"To use against you?" I ask.

When he doesn't answer, I'm a little upset he thinks I

would possibly do that. Maybe neither of us has known the other long enough to be sure of anything.

"I would never do that," I say. It is entirely up to him now whether he believes me.

We drive over a mile before he finally responds with a simple "Thank you."

"I get the feeling enough people have already done that," I say.

"It's why I stopped telling most people the truth," he says. "They're going to believe what they believe, and I'm tired of explaining. The only people I owe anything to are Abby and my mom."

"You didn't have to tell me either," I say. "You could have decided to—"

"I know," he says. "I wanted to tell you."

We drive the rest of the way back to the lot in silence, and I hope he feels less burdened now. Whenever I get painfully honest with any of my friends, I always feel a sense of lightness. That occurs only because I trust them. And he can trust me. If his sister says she forgives him, why should I hold anything against him? Especially knowing how much he regrets it.

We pull into the parking area of the tree lot. The snow-flake lights around the perimeter are turned off, but the lamp-posts are still on for security. The lights inside the trailer are off and all the curtains are shut.

"Before you leave," I say, "there is something else I need to know."

With the engine running, he turns toward me.

"When it gets closer to Christmas," I say, "will you be leaving to visit Abby and your dad?"

He looks down, but soon a smile appears on his lips. He knows I'm asking because I don't want him to leave. "This is my mom's year," he says. "Abby's coming here."

I don't want to hide my enthusiasm entirely, but I try to maintain some cool. "I'm glad," I say.

He looks at me. "I'll see my dad over spring break."

"Will he be lonely at Christmas?"

"A little," he says, "I'm sure. But another good thing about Abby living there is she forces him to get into the holiday spirit. She's taking him out to get a tree this weekend."

"She really is feisty," I say.

Caleb faces the front window. "I was looking forward to doing that with them next year," he says, "but now I don't know. I think a big part of me won't want to leave until the last minute before Christmas."

"Because of your mom?" I ask.

With every second that passes without an answer, the more weightless I feel. Is he saying he'll want to stay because of me? I want to ask—I should ask—but I'm too afraid. If he says no, I'd feel ridiculous for assuming. If he says yes, then I'd have to tell him that next year may not be like this year at all.

He steps out into the cool air and comes around to my door. He takes my hand and helps me out. We hold each other's hands a moment more, standing so close. In this instant I feel closer to him than I have with any other guy. Even though I won't be here for long. Even though I don't know when I'm returning.

I ask him to come back tomorrow. He says he will. I let go of his hand and walk toward the trailer, hoping the silence in there will calm my rushing mind.

For the past three years I've gone to school with Heather for one day before their winter break. It began as a dare during one of her movie marathons; we were curious if her school would allow it. My mom called to find out, and since the high school principal used to be a teacher at the elementary school I went to each winter, she didn't mind. "Sierra's a good kid," she said.

Heather applies eyeliner, looking into a tiny mirror stuck to the inside of her locker. "You asked him about it while eating pancakes?" she asks.

"Huge pancakes," I say. "And Rachel told me to do it somewhere public, so . . ."

"What did he say?"

I lean against the next locker. "It's not my story to tell. Just keep giving him a chance, okay?"

"I'm letting you hang out with him unchaperoned. I'd say that's giving him a chance." She caps her eyeliner. "When I heard the two of you were prancing all over town delivering Christmas trees like Mr. and Mrs. Claus, I figured the rumors must be exaggerated."

"Thank you," I say.

She shuts her locker. "So now that you two are legit, I should remind you why I encouraged a holiday fling to begin with."

We both look down the busy hall to Devon, standing in a circle of his guy friends.

"Are you over that whole Winter Queen thing?" I ask.

"Believe me, I made him grovel over that," she says. "A lot. Still, look at him! He should be standing over here with me. You'd think if he really liked me—"

"Stop!" I say. "Listen to yourself. First you want to break up, but you say you would never do that to him over the holidays. And yet when he *doesn't* give you attention, you get despondent."

"I do not get . . . ! Wait, is that like being all pouty?"

"Yes."

"Fine. I get despondent."

Everything is clear now. This has never been about Devon being dull. It's about Heather needing to feel like he wants her.

I follow her through the halls to her next class. We get stares from students and teachers who wonder who I am, or people who recognize me, realizing it's that time of year again.

"You and Devon hang out a lot," I say, "and I know you make out a lot, but does he know you really like him?"

"He knows," she says. "But I don't know if he likes *me*. I mean, he says he does. And he calls me every night, but that's to talk about fantasy football and nothing at all important, like figuring out what I might want for Christmas."

We leave the busy hall and walk into her English class.

The teacher gives me a nod and a smile, and then he points to a chair already placed beside Heather's desk.

As the tardy bell rings, Jeremiah skids into the room and takes the desk right in front of Heather. My heart beats faster. I replay that sad look on Jeremiah's face when he walked past Caleb at the parade.

While the teacher fires up the SMART Board, Jeremiah turns to me. His voice is deep. "So you're Caleb's new girlfriend."

I feel my face get warm and I freeze for a moment. "Who said that?"

"It's not a big town," he says. "And I know a lot of guys on the baseball team. Your dad's reputation is legendary."

I cover my face with my hands. "Oh, God."

He laughs. "It's all good. I'm glad you're hanging out with him. It's kind of perfect."

I drop my hands and study him carefully. The teacher says something about *A Midsummer Night's Dream* while messing with his computer, and people around us rummage through their notebooks. I lean forward and whisper, "Why is it perfect?"

He turns slightly. "Because of his tree thing. And your tree thing. It's cool."

Heather whispers at me. "Do not get me in trouble. I have to come back here tomorrow."

As discreetly as I can, I ask, "Why don't you hang out with him anymore?"

Jeremiah looks down at his desk and then tucks his chin

against his shoulder to look back at me. "He told you we were friends?"

"He told me a lot," I say. "He's a really good guy, Jeremiah."

He looks to the front of the room. "It's complicated."

"Is it?" I ask. "Or does your family make it that way?"

He winces a little and then looks at me like, *Who is this girl?*

I consider what my parents would say if they knew Caleb snapped like he did, even if it was years ago. Ever since I can remember, they have always emphasized forgiveness, believing people can change. I want to think they would stand by those words, but when it comes to me and who I like, I'm not sure how they would react.

I glance at Heather with an apologetic shrug, but this may be the only chance I get with Jeremiah. "Have you talked to them about it since?" I ask.

"They don't want this kind of problem for me," he says.

It makes me so sad—and angry—that his parents or anyone would consider Caleb a *kind* of problem. "Right, but would you be friends if you could?"

He eyes the front of the room again and the teacher futzing with his computer. Jeremiah turns back to me. "I was there. I saw how it went down. Caleb was mad as hell but I don't think he would have hurt her."

"You don't think?" I say. "You *know* he wouldn't have."

His fingers hold the sides of his desk. "I *don't* know that," he says. "And you weren't there."

The words hit hard. It has never been just Jeremiah's family. It's also him; and he's right, I wasn't there.

"So neither one of you is allowed to change, is that it?"

Heather taps my arm and I lean back in my chair. Jeremiah stares at a blank page in his notebook throughout class, but he never writes a word.

🌲

I don't see Caleb until the end of the day. He's with Luis and Brent, leaving the math wing. I watch them slap each other on the shoulders and take off in different directions. He smiles when he sees me and comes over.

"You know, most people try to get *out* of school," he says. "How was your day?"

"There were some interesting moments." I lean against a wall in the hallway. "I know you'll probably say you never used the word *arduous* in a sentence, but it was mostly that."

"I have not used that one," he says. He leans against the wall with me, pulls out his phone, and starts typing. "I'm going to look that one up later."

I laugh and then notice Heather walking toward us. Several paces behind her, Devon is talking on his phone.

"We're going downtown," she says. "Shopping. You two want to join us?"

Caleb looks at me. "It's up to you. I'm not working."

"Sure," I say to Heather. I turn to Caleb. "Let Devon drive. You can look up your word-of-the-day."

"Keep teasing me and I may not buy you a peppermint mocha," he says. Then, like it's the most natural thing he's done, he takes my hand and we follow our friends outside.

CHAPTER FOURTEEN

Caleb only lets go of my hand so that he can open the back door of Devon's car. After I'm seated, he closes the door and walks around to the other side. From the front passenger seat, Heather turns and gives me a knowing smirk.

I give her the only suitable response for a situation like this: "Shut up."

When she wiggles her eyebrows at me, I almost laugh. But I do love that she made the decision to stop questioning Caleb. Either that or she's just really happy to have us along for the ride with Devon.

When Caleb gets in, he asks, "So what are we shopping for?"

"Christmas presents," Devon says. He starts the engine and then looks at Heather. "I think. Right?"

Heather closes her eyes and leans her head against the window.

I need to feed Devon some boyfriend tips. "Okay, but who are *you* shopping for, Devon?"

"Probably my family," he says. "What about you?"

This is going to be much harder than I thought, so I change tactics. "Heather, if you could have anything for Christmas, what would it be? Anything at all."

Heather clues in to what I'm doing, and that's because she's not ridiculously oblivious like Devon. "That is a great question, Sierra. You know, I've never been someone who asked for much, so maybe . . ."

Devon messes with the radio as he drives. It takes everything I have not to kick his seat. Caleb looks out the window, close to laughing. At least he gets what's going on.

"Maybe what?" I ask Heather.

She glares directly at Devon. "Something thoughtful would be nice, like a day of doing my favorite things: a movie, a hike, maybe a picnic on Cardinals Peak. Something so easy even a moron could do it."

Devon switches the radio station again. Now I want to smack him in the back of his thick skull, but he's driving and I care too much about the other passengers.

Caleb leans forward. He puts a hand on Devon's shoulder while looking at Heather. "That sounds really fun, Heather. Maybe someone will give you that best day ever."

Devon looks into the rearview mirror at Caleb. "Did you tap me?"

Heather leans up close to his face. "We were talking about what I want for Christmas, Devon!"

Devon smiles at her. "Like one of those scented candles? You love those!"

"That's real observant," she says, sitting back. "They're only all over my dresser and desk."

Looking back to the road, Devon smiles and pats her on the knee.

Caleb and I start laughing softly, but then we can't hold back and it comes roaring out. I lean against his shoulder, dabbing tears from the corners of my eyes. Eventually Heather joins in . . . a little. Even Devon starts to laugh, though I have no idea why.

🌲

Every winter, a retired couple opens a seasonal shop downtown called the Candle Box. It's almost always in a different location—a store that would otherwise sit vacant during the holidays. They stay open about the same stretch of time as our lot, but the owners live here throughout the year. The store's festive shelves and tables are stocked with scented and decorative candles with pinecones, glitter, and other items layered into the wax. What draws some people into the store who would otherwise walk by is the candle-making in the front window.

Today the wife sits on a stool surrounded by tubs of various colors of melted wax. She dips a wick into the wax again and again to create the candle, which thickens with each dip, alternating layers of red and white. She finishes this candle with a dunk into the white wax and then hangs it on a hook using a loop in the wick. The wax is still warm as she slides a knife down the sides, peeling back strips and exposing the many tiers of white and red. About an inch from the bottom she stops slicing the wax and, in a ripple design, presses the ribbon back against the candle. That process continues, sliding the knife and rippling the ribbon, around the entire candle.

I could watch this process for hours.

Caleb, though, keeps interrupting my hypnotized state.

"Which do you like better?" he asks, lifting candles in front of my face. First he wants me to smell a jar with a picture of a coconut on the label, and then one with cranberries.

"I don't know. I've smelled too many," I say. "They all smell the same now."

"No way! Cranberries and coconuts smell nothing alike." One at a time, he holds the candles close to my nose again.

"Find something with cinnamon," I say. "I love cinnamon candles."

His mouth drops open in mock horror. "Sierra, cinnamon is a starter scent. Everyone likes cinnamon! The point is to move on to something more sophisticated."

I smirk. "Is that right?"

"Absolutely. Wait here."

I don't have a chance to get fully re-mesmerized by the candle-making before Caleb returns with another jar. He covers the picture with his hand, but the wax is a deep red.

"Close your eyes," he says. "Concentrate."

I close my eyes again.

"What does it smell like?" he asks.

Now *I* laugh. "Like someone recently brushed their teeth and is right up in my face."

He nudges my arm, and—eyes still shut—I inhale deeply. Then I open my eyes, looking directly into his. He feels so, so close. My voice comes out breathy, almost a whisper. "Tell me. I like it."

He smiles warmly. "It has some peppermint, some Christmas trees. A little chocolate, I think." The label on the jar, in scripted gold letters, says *A Very Special Christmas*. He sets the lid back on the candle. "It reminds me of you."

I wet my lips. "Do you want me to buy it for you?"

"That's a hard one," he murmurs, our faces mere inches apart. "I think I'd probably go crazy if I lit this thing in my room."

"Guys!" Devon interrupts. "Heather and I are getting pictures with that Santa in the plaza. Want to come?"

Heather must have seen the moment happening between Caleb and me. She grabs Devon's hand and pulls him back. "It's fine. We can meet them later."

"No, we'll come," Caleb says.

He holds out his hand and I take it. Really, I would love to disappear somewhere uninterrupted with him. Instead, we leave to get our picture taken while sitting on a stranger's lap.

When we get to the plaza, the line snakes out from Santa's Gingerbread Cottage, through the courtyard, and halfway around a wishing fountain with a bronze bear reaching into the water.

Devon flicks a penny and it hits the bear's paw. "Three wishes!" he says.

While Devon and Caleb talk, Heather leans close to me. "Looks like you two could've used some alone time back there."

"That's the joy of Christmas," I say. "You're always surrounded—completely—by family and friends."

When we finally get to the cottage door, a chubby guy dressed like an elf guides Devon and Heather to Santa, who is perched on an oversized red velvet throne. They squeeze together onto his lap. The man has an authentic snowy white beard, and he puts his arms around them both like they're little kids. It's silly, but adorable. I lean into Caleb's shoulder and he puts his arm around me.

"I used to love getting pictures with Santa," he says. "My parents dressed Abby and me in matching shirts and would use that year's picture for our family Christmas cards."

I wonder if memories like these are bittersweet to him now.

He looks me in the eyes and touches a finger to my forehead. "I can see your wheels spinning up there. Yes, it's okay to talk about my sister."

I smile and lean my forehead against his shoulder.

"But thank you," he says. "I love that you're trying to figure me out."

Devon and Heather walk to the register, which is staffed by another elf. When we take our turn on Santa's lap, I watch

Caleb pull the purple comb from his pocket and run it through his hair a few times.

An elf with a camera clears her throat. "Are we ready?"

"Sorry," I say, turning my gaze away from Caleb.

The elf takes several pictures. We start with some goofy faces but then lean back with our arms around Santa's shoulders. The guy playing Santa goes along with everything, his jolliness never fading. He even tosses in a "Ho, ho!" before every photo.

"I'm sorry if we're heavy," I tell him.

"You haven't cried or peed," he says. "That puts you ahead of the game."

When we hop off his lap, Santa hands us each a small wrapped candy cane. I follow Caleb toward the counter to look at our pictures on the computer screen. We choose the photo of us leaning against Santa, and Caleb buys a copy for us both. While those print, he requests a photo keychain, too.

"Really?" I say. "You're going to drive around in your manly truck with a picture of Santa on a keychain?"

"First, it's a picture of *us* with Santa," he says. "Second, it's a purple truck, making you the first person to call it manly."

Heather and Devon are waiting outside the cottage for us, with Devon's arm around her shoulders. They want to grab something to eat, so Caleb and I follow, but I have to guide him by the arm while he attaches the photo to his keyring. I successfully navigate him around one near-collision.

Then I get so distracted by his careful expression as he slides our photo onto an item he'll see every day that we walk into someone.

He drops his phone. "Oops. Sorry, Caleb."

Caleb picks up the phone and hands it back. "No problem."

We continue on and Devon whispers, "At school, that guy's always got his face in his phone. He should try looking up every once in a while."

"Are you kidding me?" Heather says. "You are the last—"

Devon holds up a hand like a shield. "I'm joking!"

"He was talking to Danielle," Caleb says. "I saw her name on his screen."

"Still?" Heather fills me in. "Danielle lives in Tennessee. He met her over the summer at theater camp, and they totally fell in love."

"Like that'll last," I say.

Caleb's eyes narrow and I wince, instantly regretting my words. I squeeze his arm tighter, but he keeps his gaze straight ahead. I feel awful, but he can't possibly think there's a real future in such a long-distance relationship. Can he?

This—Caleb and I—can only end one way, with both of us getting hurt. And we already know the date that will happen. The longer we push this thing forward, the worse that hurt will be.

So what am I doing here?

I stop. "You know what, I should really start heading back to work."

Heather steps in front of me. She can see what's going on. "Sierra . . ."

Everyone stops walking, but only Caleb refuses to look at me.

"I haven't been helping out as much as I should," I say. "And my stomach's hurting anyway so . . ."

"Do you want us to drive you back?" Devon asks.

"I'll walk with her," Caleb says. "I've lost my appetite, too."

We do most of the thirty-minute walk back to the lot in silence. He must know my stomach doesn't really hurt because he never asks if I'm okay. By the time the Bigtop comes into view, though, it does hurt. I shouldn't have said anything.

"I have a feeling all the stuff with my sister bothers you more than you admit," he says.

"That's not it at all," I say. I stop walking and take his hand. "Caleb, I am not the kind of person who would hold the past over you like that."

He runs his other hand through his hair. "Then why did you say that back there, about long-distance relationships?"

I take a deep breath. "You really think it'll work for them? I don't want to be cynical, but two lives, two sets of friends, two different states? The odds are against them from the beginning."

"You mean they're against us," he says.

I let go of his hand and look away.

"I knew that guy before he met Danielle, and I'm glad

he's with her. It's inconvenient, and he doesn't see her every day or go to dances with her, but they talk all the time." He pauses and, for a fleeting moment, his eyes narrow. "I really did not see you as a pessimist."

Pessimist? I feel my anger rising. "That proves we haven't known each other very long."

"We haven't," he says, "but I've known you long enough."

"Is that right?" I can't shake the sarcasm from my voice.

"He and Danielle have a huge roadblock, but they work around it," Caleb says. "I'm sure they know more about each other than most people. Are you saying they should only focus on the one thing that makes it difficult?"

I blink. "Are you serious? You avoid the girls around here because you don't want to deal with explaining your past to them. That's pretty focused on the difficult."

The frustration pours out of him. "That is not what I said. I told you I wasn't with anyone long enough to find out if they were worth it. But you *are* worth it. I know that."

My head swims in what he just said. "Really? You think we're possible?"

His eyes are adamant. "Yes." Soon they turn gentle and he gives me a delicate, sincere smile. "Sierra, I combed my hair for you."

I look down and laugh, and then push my hair out of my face.

He rubs his thumb along my cheek. I raise my chin toward him and hold my breath.

"My sister gets here this weekend," he says. There's a nervousness in his voice. "I want you to meet her. And my mom. Will you?"

I look deep into his eyes to answer him. "Yes." With that one word, I feel like I'm answering a dozen more questions that he no longer needs to ask.

CHAPTER FIFTEEN

When I get to the trailer, I collapse on my bed. I set the picture of Caleb and me with Santa on the table, gazing at it sideways while I rest my head on the ugly-sweater pillow.

Then I leap to my knees and hold our picture up to my frames from back home. First I show it to Elizabeth. In my best Elizabeth voice, I ask, "Why are you doing this? You're there to sell trees and hang out with Heather."

I answer, "I have been, but—"

I switch back to Elizabeth. "This can't go anywhere, Sierra, no matter what he says about focusing on the possible."

I squeeze my eyes shut. "I don't know, you guys. Maybe it could."

I move on to Rachel's picture. The first thing she does is whistle and point out his dimple.

"I know," I say. "Trust me, that does not make it any easier."

"What's the worst that can happen?" she says. "You get your heart broken. So? It sounds like that's going to happen anyway."

I drop back onto my bed, clutching Caleb's picture to my chest. "I know."

I go outside to see if I can help in the Bigtop. Things are slow, so I mix hot chocolate in my Easter egg mug and head back to the trailer for schoolwork. Passing our tallest Fraser firs, I see Andrew tugging a garden hose between them. After our blowup the other day, I decide to make nice for the sake of working together.

"Thanks for always checking their water," I say. "They look good."

Andrew completely ignores me. He twists the nozzle on the hose and starts misting the trees. So much for staying cordial.

In the trailer, I pull out my laptop and review a chapter write-up I threw together late last night. Checking my email, I see Monsieur Cappeau is upset I blew off our last conversation, so I reschedule it and then shut everything down.

Peeking through the curtains I watch Dad approach Andrew, motioning for him to pass him the hose. He demonstrates the way he wants the trees misted and then hands it back. Andrew nods and Dad smiles, patting him on the shoulder. Then he walks into our forest of trees. Instead of resuming misting, Andrew quickly looks over to the trailer.

I snap back, letting the curtain close.

I decide to make dinner for the family, slicing up vegetables from McGregor's and cooking them together in a large pot of soup. While that simmers, I watch another flatbed loaded with trees pull up outside. Uncle Bruce hops down from the cab. While some of our workers swarm the truck and climb the ladder to the trees, Uncle Bruce jogs over to the trailer and opens the door.

"Wow, it smells great in here!" He pulls me into a bear hug. "Out there, it smells like tree sap and teenage boys."

He excuses himself and ducks into the bathroom while I check on the soup. I sprinkle in a few spices from the cupboard and then stir it with a wooden spoon. Uncle Bruce returns to have a taste before heading back out to the trees. I lean against the counter and stare at the door as it closes behind him. These are the moments that make me look forward to doing this for the rest of my life. When my parents get too old, it will be up to me to decide the fate of our farm and whether we run any lots.

When the truck bed is empty, Dad stays outside to direct the workers, but Mom and Uncle Bruce come in and join me. They're so thrilled with the soup, slurping it up like hungry wolves, they say nothing about me bailing on the heavy labor.

Ladling himself a second bowl, Uncle Bruce tells us about Aunt Penny wrapping their whole Christmas tree in lights without plugging them in first. "Who does that?" he says. When she finally turned them on, half of the lights didn't work, so now they've got a tree half as bright as it could be.

After Uncle Bruce goes outside to take over for Dad, Mom heads into the tiny bedroom for a short nap before the evening rush. Dad comes in and I hold out a bowl of soup for him. He stands just inside the door, seemingly agitated, like he wants to talk to me about something. Instead, he shakes his head and walks to the bedroom.

The next afternoon, when things slow down, I return a call to Rachel.

"You are not going to believe what happened!" she says.

"Some actor saw your post about the winter formal and accepted?"

"Hey, they do that sometimes—it's good press—so I'm still holding out hope," she says. "But this is way better than that."

"So spill!"

"The girl in *A Christmas Carol*, the one playing the Ghost of Christmas Past, she has mono! I mean, that's not good. But I'm going to replace her, which is!"

I laugh. "At least you recognize mono isn't good."

Rachel laughs, too. "I know, I know, but it's mono, not cancer. Anyway, I know it's last minute, but Sunday night's the only show that isn't sold out."

"As in . . . tomorrow?" I ask.

"I already looked it up, and you can hop a train at midnight and—"

"Midnight tonight?"

"You'll get here in plenty of time," she says.

I must have paused too long because Rachel asks if I'm still here.

"I'll ask," I say, "but I can't promise."

"No, of course," she says, "but try. I want to see you. Elizabeth does, too. And you can stay at my house. I already asked my parents. And then you can give us the scoop on Caleb. You've been way too quiet on that front . . ."

"We had the talk about his sister," I say. "I think he told me everything."

"So I'm guessing he's not a knife-wielding psychopath?"

"I haven't said much to anyone because it still feels complicated," I say. "I'm not sure how I feel, or even how I want to feel."

"That's confusing to hear," Rachel says. "It must be really confusing to think."

"Now that I know it's not wrong to like him," I say, "I obsess over whether that makes it right. I'm only here for a couple more weeks."

"Hmm . . ." I can hear Rachel tapping the side of her phone. "Sounds like you don't expect to forget him when you leave."

"At this point, I don't know if that's possible."

After we end the call, I find Mom in the Bigtop hanging up newly made wreaths. Over her work shirt she wears a dark green apron that says *It's Beginning to Smell a Lot like Christmas*. Last year we gave that apron to Dad on Christmas Eve. We always get him something cheesy before going home, where the real presents are.

I help her fluff up some of the branches within the wreaths. Eventually I blurt out, "Can I take a train and see Rachel be the Ghost of Christmas Past on Sunday?"

Mom freezes while adjusting a wreath. "I think you said something about Rachel and a ghost, or . . ."

"It's terrible timing," I say, "I know. This weekend is going to be so busy here. I don't need to go if it'll be an inconvenience to anyone." I don't mention not particularly wanting to go. I don't want to waste two potential days with Caleb stuck on a train by myself.

She walks to a sealed cardboard box set on the counter and slices through the tape with a razor. "I'll talk to your dad," she says. "We may be able to work something out."

"Oh . . ."

After opening the box, she hands me several thin white boxes of silver tinsel. I set those on the shelf below the wreaths, and then she hands me more.

"A few of the workers have been asking for more hours," she says. "We can staff up for a few days while you're gone." She sets the empty box below the counter and wipes her hands on her apron. "Can you watch the register for me?"

That means she's going to talk to Dad.

"Actually," I say, closing my eyes, "I don't really want to go." I smile at her with gritted teeth.

Mom chuckles. "Then why did you ask?"

I scrub a hand over my face. "Because I thought you'd say no. I thought you'd need me here. But I told Rachel I would ask."

Mom's face turns soft. "Honey, what's going on? You know your father and I love having you here to help, but we would never want you to feel like you gave up everything for the family business."

"But it is a *family* business," I say. "One day I could take it over."

"We would love that, of course," Mom says. She pulls me into a hug and then leans back so we can see each other. "But if I'm reading you correctly, we're not just talking about the family business or a play."

I look away. "Rachel's important to me. You know that. Even though the Ghost of Christmas Past doesn't even talk, I'd still love to see it. But . . . well . . . Caleb asked me to meet his family this weekend."

Mom studies my expression. "If I was your dad, I'd be booking that train ticket right now."

"I know," I say. "Am I being stupid?"

"Your feelings are not stupid," she says. "But I need to tell you, your dad has some real reservations about Caleb."

I frown. "Can you tell me why?"

"I told him we need to trust you," Mom says, "but I can't say I'm not a little concerned myself."

"Mom, tell me," I say, searching her eyes. "Did Andrew say something?"

"He talked to your father," she says. "And so should you."

"But it's *A Christmas Carol*!" Rachel says.

I lay on my bed with the phone to my ear and one hand on my forehead. Rachel's photo looks down on me as she pretends to hide from paparazzi. "It's not that I don't want to see it," I tell her. I could say my parents won't let me leave, but she and I have always been honest with each other.

"Then get on the train!" she says. "I swear, if this is about that boy—"

"His name is Caleb. And yes, it is. Rachel, I'm supposed to meet his family this weekend. After that, we only have a few days before—" I hear a click. "Are you there?"

I slam my phone on the table, put the ugly-sweater pillow over my mouth, and scream. Giving myself a moment to be angry, I decide to use the energy to confront Dad about what Andrew said to him.

I find Dad carrying a small tree out to a car.

"No, there's too much going on tonight," he says. The bluntness of his tone tells me he's just not ready to talk. "Your mom and I have to review sales, and . . . No, Sierra, I can't."

When Heather calls to see if we can make cookies tonight with the guys, I don't even bother asking. Mom said she doesn't want the family business intruding on my life, so when Devon pulls up, I tell her I'm leaving, hop into his car, and we go.

We pull into the supermarket parking lot and Caleb leans forward. He asks Devon to park at the opposite end from the Hoppers' Christmas tree lot so there's no awkward conversation about why he hasn't been around lately.

"You should buy from them, too," I say. "I love the Hopper family. I mean, then I would have to rescind your discount, but . . ."

Heather laughs. "Sierra, I think you'll have to tell him what *rescind* means."

"Ha. Funny," Caleb says. "I know what it means . . . in context."

My phone pings with a text from Elizabeth, and I cover the screen with my hand to read it. She tells me I need to consider which friends will be here years from now. Obviously, Rachel called her once she hung up on me. A second text from Elizabeth expresses disappointment that I'm doing this over a guy I barely know.

"Everything all right?" Caleb asks.

I turn off my phone and put it in my pocket. "Just some drama in Oregon," I say.

Especially coming from Elizabeth, those texts feel aggressive. Do they think my decision was easy? Or that Caleb can't possibly matter to me? It's not easy, and I am not becoming one of those girls. I'm here for a short time, and I don't want to erase several days from the calendar that I could spend with him.

We get out of the car and Caleb exaggerates flipping up his collar and scrunching down so Mr. Hopper won't notice him. Even though we're too far away for him to see us, I do the same, and we run into the store.

Heather folds the shopping list in half and then tears it along the crease. She gives half the list to me and Caleb, keeps half for herself, and then loops arms with Devon. We agree to meet at register eight when we're done. Caleb and I start by heading toward the dairy section at the back of the store.

"You seemed out of it when we picked you up," Caleb says. "Is everything okay?"

I can only shrug. Things are not okay. Rachel's mad that I'm not coming to her show. Dad would be mad that I'm here right now.

"That's all I get? A shrug?" Caleb asks. "Thanks. That's A+ for communication."

I don't want to talk about this while shopping, so now Caleb is upset with me. He walks a full step ahead. When we reach the wall of refrigerated milk, he abruptly stops and reaches back for my hand.

I follow his gaze until I spot Jeremiah setting a gallon of milk in a shopping cart. When a woman who looks like his mom wheels the cart around, we all face each other. I give his mom a closer look. I recognize her—she came to the lot a few days ago. When I offered to help, she mumbled something about our prices and walked right past me.

Jeremiah gives both of us courtesy smiles.

His mom begins to push the cart around us. "Caleb," she says, instead of "Hello." Her voice is tight.

Caleb's voice is soft. "Hi, Mrs. Moore." Before she can pass, he adds, "This is my friend Sierra."

Mrs. Moore looks at me, still pushing the cart past us. "Nice to meet you, dear."

I meet her gaze. "My parents own one of the Christmas tree lots," I say. I step in the same direction they're heading and she stops the cart. "I think you came by recently."

Her smile is hesitant and she looks at Jeremiah. "Which reminds me, we still need to get ours."

I feel the tension in Caleb's hand, but I do my best to ignore him and continue the conversation. I follow beside their cart, pulling Caleb with me. "Come by again," I say. "My uncle brought down a whole new shipment. They're really fresh."

Mrs. Moore looks back at Caleb again, with less coldness, but turns to me to speak. "Maybe we will. It was nice to meet you, Sierra." She pushes the cart ahead, and Jeremiah follows her down the aisle.

Caleb's eyes look glazed. I squeeze his arm to show that I'm here, but also to apologize if I forced that moment on him. But it's clear to me that he and Jeremiah should not have stopped being friends.

Before I can express any of this to him, there's an angry voice behind us. "My brother doesn't need your mess, Caleb. He's good."

I wheel around. Jeremiah's sister stands with her hands on her hips, waiting for Caleb to react, but he says nothing. When his gaze drops to the floor, I take a step toward her.

"What's your name?" I say. "It's Cassandra, right? Listen, Cassandra, Caleb is good, too. You and your brother should learn that."

She looks from me to Caleb, probably wondering why he's not sticking up for himself. I tilt my head, ready to ask her the same thing about Jeremiah.

"I don't know you," Cassandra says to me, "and you don't know my brother."

"But I do know Caleb," I say.

She shakes her head. "He is not getting mixed up in that. Not again." She takes off down the aisle.

I squeeze Caleb's hand as we watch her disappear around the corner. "I am so sorry," I whisper. "I know you can stick up for yourself. I just couldn't stop."

"People will think what they want," he says. The confrontation over, I can see his calmness slowly returning. Over the years, he's clearly learned to let these moments wash off his back, and now he smirks at me. "So, did you get it out of your system?"

"I was ready to take swings if it came to that," I say.

"And now you know why I didn't let go of your hand."

Heather and Devon come up behind us. He's carrying a basket with eggs, frosting, and sprinkles.

"Can we please go make cookies now?" she asks. She looks at our hands. "Where's all your stuff? It was a short list!"

After gathering our items we walk to the checkout line together. Jeremiah, his mom, and Cassandra are two registers over. None of them acknowledge us, but the way they look everywhere *but* at us says everything.

"Doesn't it bother you that he won't even look at you?" I ask Caleb.

"Of course it does," he says. "But it's my fault, so let it go."

"Are you kidding me?" I say. "It's the three of them who should—"

"Please," he says. "Let it go."

I allow Caleb, Heather, and Devon to put things on the conveyor belt while I glare at Jeremiah's family. Mrs. Moore looks over and does a double-take, obviously uneasy that I'm watching her.

"Come by tomorrow!" I shout. "We're giving friends and family a discount."

Cassandra narrows her eyes at me but keeps her mouth shut. Caleb pretends to be occupied with the gum rack.

Devon looks confused. "Can I get a discount?"

In the morning, I'm surprised when Jeremiah actually shows up at the lot with Cassandra. He looks like he just rolled out of bed, threw on sweatpants, a hoodie, and a ball cap. She looks like she woke up to an alarm, had coffee, breakfast, did her hair and makeup, and then got him up.

Jeremiah goes to investigate trees while Cassandra comes into the Bigtop.

"I'm assuming you came for the discount," I say.

"My mom wouldn't let us pass it up," she grumbles, but I'm sure Cassandra tried.

"You're welcome," I tell her.

She lowers her head a bit, but still looks me in the eyes. "So why did you offer the discount?"

"Honestly, I was hoping your parents would be standing here so I could talk to them."

She crosses her arms. "What could you say that hasn't already been covered?"

"That Caleb would never would hurt anyone," I say. "I get the feeling that hasn't been covered."

"You believe that?"

"Completely."

Cassandra laughs. "You have got to be kidding me. Jeremiah watched him go after his sister with a knife!"

"I know. I also know that he regrets it every day," I say. "He lives with it every day. His family lives with it."

Cassandra looks down and shakes her head. "My parents will never be okay with—"

"I get that, but maybe they're overdoing this protective thing," I say. "My dad makes any guy who works here clean outhouses if he even looks at me funny."

"This is a little different than flirting with someone. You know that, right?"

Behind her, Jeremiah walks into the Bigtop. He holds a tree tag in his hand but stays back from the conversation.

"I also don't think it's just your parents," I say. "Jeremiah and Caleb used to be best friends, and they should still be best friends. They just never had a chance to figure things out before these lines were drawn."

I wait for a response that doesn't come. She looks at her nails, but at least she's still here.

"You must see him at school," I say. "Everything he does proves who he is now. Did you know he delivers Christmas trees to needy families? Do you know why? Because it makes them happy."

She finally looks at me. "Or is it because he ruined his own family?"

I flinch.

She looks down and closes her eyes. "I shouldn't have said that."

I don't know what to say. In a way, maybe she's right. Caleb doesn't give the trees hoping for gold stars. He's hoping for peace, to balance his mistakes.

Jeremiah approaches. He puts a hand on his sister's shoulder. "Everything all right here?"

She turns to him. "What if it happened again, Jeremiah? What if someone pushes his buttons when you're with him and he freaks out again? You think you'll avoid getting dragged into that?"

"He made a mistake, and he's paid for it," I say. "All this time later, it still devastates him. Do you like being a part of that?"

She looks at Jeremiah. "Mom would never approve."

Jeremiah looks at me. Without accusation, he says, "You think you know him."

"I do," I say. "I know who he is now."

"I'm sorry," Cassandra says. She looks from her brother to me. "I know you want this to be different, but I will always put my brother first."

She turns and walks out of the Bigtop.

CHAPTER SIXTEEN

I watch Cassandra and Jeremiah get into their car, which now has a discounted tree strapped to the roof. Jeremiah has the passenger window down, his arm hanging out, and offers me a weary wave as they pull out of the lot.

He looks like I feel, but a part of me holds on to hope that the conversation will continue. One day, maybe someone will listen.

"What was that about?" Mom asks.

"It's complicated," I say.

"What is? Is this about Caleb, too?"

"Can we not talk about this?" I ask.

"Sierra, you need to talk to your father," Mom says. "I keep telling him to trust what you're doing, but if you can't be open with me, I won't do that anymore. Andrew told him—"

"I don't care what Andrew said," I tell her. "And you shouldn't, either."

She crosses her arms. "That defensiveness worries me, Sierra. Do you really understand what you're getting involved with here?"

I close my eyes and exhale. "Mom, what would you say is the difference between gossip and relevant information?"

She considers this. "I'd say if the people you tell aren't directly involved in any way, that's gossip."

I bite at my lower lip. "The reason I do want to tell you is because I don't want you judging Caleb based on what Andrew said, because I guarantee he didn't say it for your benefit. He said it to hurt Caleb, or to get back at me for turning him down."

Now I can tell I'm really freaking her out. "That sounds like another story I need you to tell me." She instructs me to find Dad while she gets someone to cover the register.

In the parking area, Dad and Andrew load a tree into the trunk of a woman's car. Half of the tree sticks out from the trunk, so they use twine to keep the lid from flying up. The lady offers Dad a tip but he motions for her to give it to Andrew. After Andrew accepts the tip, he follows Dad back into the lot.

"Hey, honey," Dad says. He stops in front of me and Andrew stops with him.

I look at Andrew and point my thumb over my shoulder. "You can keep working."

Andrew gives a smug smile as he walks away. He knows he's causing trouble. I guess that's what you do when you like someone who doesn't like you back.

"Sierra, that wasn't necessary," Dad says.

I suppress a well-deserved eye roll. "That's why we need to talk."

Mom, Dad, and I walk along Oak Boulevard leading away from the lot. Cars drive by and occasionally a biker pedals past. I take a deep breath and swing my arms, mustering the courage to begin this conversation. Once I start, it comes flowing out, and they let me say it all without interjecting. I tell them everything I know about Caleb, and about his family, and Jeremiah, and what Caleb does with the trees. For some reason, it takes me longer to get the story out than when Caleb told me. Maybe that's because I feel the need to add so much more about who Caleb is now.

When I'm done, Dad's frown is even deeper. "When I heard that Caleb attacked his—"

"He didn't attack her!" I say. "He went after her, but he never would've—"

"And you want me to be okay with that?" Dad says. "It was so hard to let you spend time with that boy after hearing what he did, but I wanted to trust you. I thought you had common sense, Sierra, but now I'm worried you're being naïve, making light of something that—"

"I'm being honest with you," I say. "Doesn't that count for anything?"

"Honey," Mom says, "*you* didn't tell us. Andrew did."

Dad looks at Mom. "Our daughter is dating a boy who attacked"—he holds up his hand to keep me from interrupting—"a boy who went after his sister with a knife."

"So there's no room for mercy?" I say. "Great lesson, Dad. You mess up once, you're screwed for life."

Dad points a finger at me. "That is not—"

Mom intervenes. "Sierra, we're here for one more week. If this makes your father so uncomfortable, is it something you really need to continue?"

I stop walking. "That's not the point! I didn't know Caleb back when it happened, and you didn't either. But I really like who he is now, and you should, too."

They've both stopped walking but Dad looks out into the street, his arms crossed. "Pardon me for not wanting my only child going out with a boy who I know has a violent past."

"If you didn't know what happened years ago and you only knew him now," I say, "you would be begging me to marry him."

Mom's mouth drops. I know I took that a little too far, but my frustration with the conversation is rising by the second.

"You met Mom while working at this very same lot," I say. "Do you think any of your reaction is because you're afraid of that happening to me?"

Mom holds her heart. "I can promise I never even thought of that."

Dad remains looking at the street, but his eyes are wide. "And I can say my heart just stopped."

"I hate this," I say. "He's been labeled this . . . *thing* . . . by so many people for so long. And they'd rather believe the worst of it than talk to him about it. Or just forgive him."

"If he had *used* the knife," Mom says, "there would be no way we'd even—"

"I know," I say. "I wouldn't, either."

With every car that passes, I swing between thinking I won them over and lost them completely.

"But I've also been raised to believe that everyone can become better," I say.

Still facing away, Dad says, "And it would be wrong to get in the way of that."

"Yes."

Mom takes Dad's hand and they look at each other. Without words, together they figure out where they stand. Finally, they turn to me.

"Not knowing him like you do," Dad says, "I'm sure you realize why hearing what happened with his sister makes us uncomfortable. And I would love to give him a chance, but it's hard to understand why, when we won't even be here in two weeks . . ."

He won't say it, but he wants to know why I can't just drop things. Why do I need to make them worry?

"There's no reason to worry," I say. "You said it yourself, I *do* know him. And you know you taught me to be cautious about these things. You don't have to trust him, just don't judge him. And trust me."

Dad sighs. "Do you have to get this deeply involved?"

"It looks like she already has," Mom says quietly.

Dad looks down at his hands, holding on to Mom's. He looks at me, but his eyes can only hold mine for a moment. He lets go of Mom's hands and starts heading back to the lot.

Mom and I watch him walk away.

"I think we've all expressed what we're feeling," she says. She gives my hand a squeeze and doesn't let go while we walk back to the lot together.

Every time I give Caleb the benefit of the doubt, he proves himself. Every time I stand up for him, I know I'm right. There have been a million reasons why I could have given up, but every time I don't, it makes me want to try that much harder to make us work.

That evening it takes me way too long to get ready for dinner with Caleb's family. I change my outfit three times, ending up in jeans and a cream cashmere sweater, which of course is what I started with. When there's a knock at the door, I blow my hair out of my face and give myself one last look. I open the door to find Caleb smiling up at me. He wears dark blue jeans and a black sweater with a gray bar across the chest.

He starts to say something, but then stops and looks me over. If his gaze lingers one more second I will need him to say *anything*, but he whispers, "You're beautiful."

I feel my cheeks warm. "You don't need to say that."

"I do," he says. "Whether you can take a compliment or not, you're beautiful."

I meet his eyes and smile.

"You're welcome," he says. He offers his hand to help me down and then we walk toward his truck. I don't see Dad, but Mom's helping a customer in the trees. When she looks over, I point toward the parking area so she knows I'm leaving.

Andrew restocks the netting around the tree barrel and I feel his gaze track us across the lot.

"Hang on," I tell Caleb.

He looks back at Andrew, who is now blatantly glaring at us. "Let's just go," Caleb says. "It doesn't matter."

"It matters to me," I say.

Caleb lets go of my hand and continues to his truck. He gets in and shuts the door, and I wait to make sure he's not leaving. He impatiently motions for me to do what I need to do, so I turn around and march up to Andrew.

He continues working on the netting and refuses to look at me. "Date night?"

"I talked to my parents about Caleb," I say. "Of course, I didn't get to tell them when I wanted to, but when I had to . . . because of you."

"And yet they're still letting you go," he says. "That's great parenting."

"Because they trust me over you," I say, "as they should."

He looks me in the eyes. There's so much hate inside. "They had a right to know their daughter's dating a . . . whatever he is."

My fury builds. "This is none of your business," I say. "*I'm* none of your business."

Caleb comes up behind me and takes my hand. "Sierra, come on."

Andrew looks at both of us with disgust. "Wherever you go, I hope they don't serve anything that needs cutting. For both of your sakes."

Caleb lets go of my hands. "What, so there are no knives?" he asks. "That's clever."

I see Dad move out from between two trees, watching us. Mom walks toward him, worried, and he shakes his head.

Caleb's jaw tightens and he looks away, like he could snap at any second and punch Andrew. The angry part of me wants that, but I need Caleb to stay cool. I want to know he can do that, and I want my parents to see it.

He flexes his fingers and then roughly rubs the back of his neck. He looks at Andrew, but no one says anything. Andrew looks afraid, one hand gripped to the netting like it's the only thing that keeps him from backing away. Seeing Andrew's fear, Caleb's expression shifts from angry to apologetic. He takes my hand again, lacing our fingers together, and leads me to his truck.

We sit in silence for a few minutes, both of us calming down. I feel like I should say something, but I don't know where or how to begin. Eventually, he starts the engine.

The lot recedes in the rearview mirror and Caleb breaks our silence, telling me he picked up Abby from the train station three hours ago. He looks at me and smiles. "She can't wait to meet you."

I realize Caleb hasn't told me much about how things are between them. Is it better now that she's with her dad? Are things tense when she returns?

"My mom can't wait to meet you, either," he says. "She's been bugging me about it since I met you."

"Really?" I can't hide my smile. "Since we met?"

He shrugs like it's no big deal, but the smirk gives him away. "I may have mentioned a certain girl at the lot after I brought home our tree."

I wonder what he could have possibly said about me without the opportunity to gush about any dimples.

His house is a three-minute drive off the highway. When we enter a residential area, I sense him growing more nervous. I don't know if it's his sister or his mom or me, but he's a wreck by the time we pull to the curb. The house is two stories, but narrow. A Christmas tree in the front window is lit with colored lights and topped with a golden star.

"The thing is," he says, "I've never brought anyone home like this."

"Not like what?" I ask.

He cuts the engine and looks at the house, then at me. "How would you classify what we're doing? Are we dating, are we . . . ?"

His nervousness is adorable.

"This may be a shock coming from me," I say, "but sometimes it's okay not to define everything."

He looks down at the space between us. I hope he doesn't think I'm pulling back.

"Let's not worry about finding a word for us," I say. "We're with each other."

"*With* is good," he says, but his smile is thin. "I'm most worried about the time we have left, though."

I think about the text I sent last night, telling Rachel to break a leg at tonight's performance. She still hasn't responded. I called Elizabeth, but that hasn't been returned either. He's right to be worried. *I'm* worried. How long can anyone be in two places at once?

He pops open his door. "Might as well get started."

We reach the front step and he takes my hand. His palms are sweating and his fingers are fidgety. This is not the cool, smooth guy I met that first day. He drops my hand to rub his palms along his jeans. Then he opens the door.

"They're here!" squeals a voice from upstairs.

Abby skips down the steps, looking much more confident and beautiful than I did as a freshman. What is so annoyingly cute is that she and Caleb have matching dimples. I bite my cheek to keep from pointing this out because I'm sure they've noticed. When she reaches the landing, she extends her hand. For the briefest moment as our hands touch, my mind flashes through everything I imagined happening that day between her and Caleb.

"It is so nice to finally meet you," she says. Her smile is as kind and genuine as her brother's. "Caleb's told me so much about you. I feel like I'm meeting a celebrity!"

"I . . ." I don't know what to say. "Well, okay! It's so nice to meet you, too."

Caleb's mom comes out of the kitchen with a similar smile, but no dimple. At first glance, by the way she holds herself, she seems more reserved than her children.

"Don't let Caleb keep you by the door," she says. "Come in. I hope you like lasagna."

Abby swings around the banister on her way to the kitchen. "I also hope you can eat a lot of it," she says.

Caleb's mom watches Abby walk into the kitchen. She keeps staring in that direction even after her daughter is out of view. Eventually, she lowers her head a moment, and then turns toward us. More to herself, she says, "It's nice when she's home."

With those words, I'm overwhelmed with the feeling that I shouldn't be here. Their family deserves to share this first night together without a stranger taking attention away from them. I glance at Caleb, and he must sense that I need to talk.

"I'm going to give Sierra a little tour before dinner," he says. "Is that okay?"

His mom waves us away. "We'll set the table."

She walks into the kitchen, where Abby is pulling a small table away from the wall. She touches Abby's hair as she passes, and my heart breaks.

I follow Caleb into the living room. Deep maroon curtains are pulled back, framing the Christmas tree.

"Everything okay?" he asks.

"Your mom has so little time with the two of you together," I say.

"You're not interrupting anything," he says. "I want you to meet them. That's important, too."

I can hear Caleb's mom and Abby talking in the kitchen. Their voices sound cheery. They're so happy to be together. When I look at Caleb, he's staring at the tree, his eyes incredibly sad.

I step close to the tree and look at the ornaments. You can tell a lot from the ornaments on a family's tree. This one is a mishmash of things he and Abby must've made when they were small, plus some fancy ornaments from locations all over the world.

I touch a twinkling Eiffel Tower. "Did your mom visit all these places?"

He nudges a Sphinx wearing a Santa hat. "You know how collections start. One of her friends brings back an ornament from Egypt, another friend sees it on our tree and brings back something from her trip."

"She's got some globe-trotting friends," I say. "Does she ever go anywhere?"

"Not since the split," he says. "At first, it was because we didn't have enough money."

"And then?"

He looks toward the kitchen. "When one child decides to leave, I guess it's harder to leave the other for even a short time."

I touch an ornament of what I assume is the Leaning Tower of Pisa, but it dangles straight up and down on the tree. "Couldn't you go with her?"

He laughs. "And now we're back to the money issue."

Caleb leads me upstairs to see his room. He walks ahead of me down the narrow hall toward an open door at the other end, but my legs stop fast at a closed door painted solid white. I lean in close and my breath catches. A series of painted-over cut-marks are clustered at eye level. Instinctively, I feel them with my fingertips.

I hear the breath rush out of Caleb. I look over and see him watching me.

"The door used to be painted red," he says. "My mom tried to sand it down and paint over them so they're less obvious, but . . . there they are."

What happened that night now feels so real. Now I know he ran from the kitchen and up a flight of stairs. His sister cried behind this door while Caleb stood right here, striking it over and over with the blade of a knife. Caleb—gentler than anyone I've met—went after Abby with a knife. And he did it while his best friend watched. I can't merge that version of him with the one watching me right now. From the doorway of his room, his expression is locked somewhere between worry and shame. I want to tell him that I'm not freaked out, to hold on to him and reassure him. But I can't.

His mom calls from below, "You two ready to eat?"

Our eyes don't leave each other. The door of his room is open, but I won't be stepping inside there. Not right now. Now, we need to get back to normal, or as close as we can, for his mom and Abby. He walks by me, letting his fingers graze my hand, but he doesn't take it. I take one more look at his sister's door and then follow him down the stairs.

Colorful ceramic plates hang on the kitchen walls. A small table in the center of the floor is set for the four of us. While our kitchen back home is bigger than theirs, this feels cozier.

"The table isn't usually in the middle of the floor," his mom says, standing beside her chair, "but there aren't usually so many of us."

"Your kitchen's way more spacious than the trailer where I'm living." I stretch out my arms. "I'd be in the bathroom and the microwave if I did this."

His mom laughs and then walks to the stove. When she opens the oven door, the room fills with the delicious smell of melted cheese, tomato sauce, and garlic.

Caleb holds out a chair for me and I thank him while I sit. He slides into the chair to my right, but then jumps up and pulls out the chair for his sister, too. Abby laughs and swats him, and I can tell from the easy way she is around him that she really has let go of their past.

Caleb's mom brings a pan of lasagna to the table and places it in the middle. When she sits, she sets a napkin on her lap. "We do family-style, Sierra. Go ahead and serve yourself first."

Caleb reaches for the spatula. "I got this." He dishes me out a massive chunk of lasagna, oozing cheese, and then he does the same for Abby and his mom.

"You forgot yourself," I say.

Caleb looks at his empty plate and then cuts a piece for himself. Abby puts an elbow on the table, covering a smile while she watches her brother.

"So you're a freshman?" I say. "How do you like high school so far?"

"She's doing great," Caleb says. "I mean, you are, right?"

I tilt my head and look at him. Maybe he feels a need to prove everything's fine after our moment at the door upstairs.

Abby shakes her head at him. "Yes, dear brother, I'm doing fantastic. I'm happy and it's a good school."

I turn to her and smile. "Is Caleb a bit overprotective?"

She rolls her eyes. "He's like the happiness police, always calling to make sure my life's going well."

"Abby," Caleb's mom says, "let's have a nice dinner, okay?"

"That's what I was trying to do," Abby says.

Caleb's mom looks at me, but her smile looks anxious. She turns to Abby. "I don't think we need to bring up certain things when there are guests."

Caleb puts his hand on mine. "Mom, she was just answering a question."

I give Caleb's hand a squeeze and then look over at Abby. Her eyes are lowered.

After a good minute of eating in silence, his mom starts asking questions about what it's like to live on a Christmas tree farm. Abby is in awe of how much land we own when I try to describe what it looks like. I almost tell her she should come visit, but I'm sure either answer would lead to more awkward silence. The whole family looks shocked when I tell them about Uncle Bruce's helicopter and how I hook trees to it while it's flying.

Caleb's mom looks between him and Abby. "I cannot imagine letting either of you do that."

Caleb finally appears to be relaxing. We share stories about the trees we've delivered together, and he tells about some he did on his own. Whenever Caleb speaks, I notice his mom looks at Abby. Does she wonder, while Abby listens to the stories, what it would be like for them to still grow up together? When I tell them it was my idea to bring the families homemade cookies, I catch Caleb's mom winking at him and my heart speeds up a little. When we're done eating, no one makes a move to leave the table.

But then Abby talks about getting a tree with her dad. Their mom goes around collecting plates, and Abby starts talking directly to me. I hold her gaze, but I can see Caleb looking down at his hands on the table while his mom puts things in the dishwasher.

Their mom stays away from the table until Abby's story is done. She then brings over a plate full of Rice Krispies treats with baked-in red and green sprinkles. Abby asks me if it's hard to be away from home and all my friends for an entire month every year. We all grab a treat and I consider her question.

"I do miss my friends," I say, "but it's been like this since I was born. I guess when you've grown up one way, it's hard to miss how things could be different, you know?"

"Unfortunately," Caleb says, "in Abby's case, we know how things could be different."

I hold on to his arm. "That is not what I meant."

Caleb sets down his dessert. "You know what, I'm exhausted." He looks at me, a flash of pain in his eyes. "We shouldn't make your parents worry."

It's like a bucket of ice water drops over me.

Caleb stands up, avoiding everyone's eyes, and then pushes in his chair. I numbly stand up from mine. I thank his mom and Abby for the nice dinner, and his mom looks down at her plate. Abby shakes her head at Caleb, but no words need to be said. He walks toward the front door and I follow.

We walk out into the cool night. Halfway to his truck, I grab Caleb's arm and stop him. "I was having a nice time in there."

He won't look me in the eyes. "I saw where things were going."

I want him to look at me, but he can't. He stands there, eyes closed, rubbing his hand through his hair. Then he walks to his truck and lets himself in. I get in on my side and shut the door. He has the key in the ignition but hasn't turned it yet, his gaze locked on the steering wheel.

"It feels like everything's okay with Abby," I say. "Your mom misses her, obviously, but the person who seemed the most uncomfortable in there was you."

He starts the truck. "Abby's forgiven me, and that helps. But I cannot forgive myself for everything I took from my mom. That was lost because of me, which is hard to forget with Abby sitting right there and you talking about home."

He puts his truck in drive, turns us in the opposite direction, and we both stay silent the entire way to the lot. The lot is still open as we pull into the parking area. I see several customers browsing and Dad carrying a newly flocked tree to the Bigtop. If this night had gone like I had hoped, we would be returning with this place closed for the night. We would sit in his truck, parked, and talk about what a beautiful evening this was, and maybe then we would finally kiss.

Instead, he pulls into a dimly lit spot of the parking area and I let myself out. Caleb stays in the driver's seat, his hands not leaving the wheel. I stand outside my open door, staring at him.

He still can't face me. "I'm sorry, Sierra. You don't deserve this. When I see you here, we've got Andrew. And you saw what my house is like. We can't even go to a grocery store without drama. That's not going to change in the time we have left."

I can't believe what he's saying. He couldn't even look at me to say it. "And yet, I'm still here," I say.

"It's too much." He looks me in the eyes now. "I hate having you see it all."

My body feels weak, and I touch the door for balance. "You said I was worth it. I believed you."

He doesn't answer.

"What hurts me most," I say, "is that you're worth it, too.

179

Until you realize that's all that matters, it will always be too much."

He stares at his steering wheel. "I can't do it anymore," he says softly.

I wait for him to take that back. He doesn't know all I've done to stand up for him. With Heather. My parents. Jeremiah. I even angered my friends back home so I could be with him. If he knew any of that, though, it would only hurt him more.

I leave without shutting the door and walk to the trailer without looking back. I keep the lights off inside, drop onto my bed, and muffle my cries into the pillow. I want to talk to someone, but Heather is out with Devon. And for the first time, I can't call Rachel or Elizabeth back home.

I pull aside the curtain above my bed and look out. His truck hasn't left. The passenger door is still open. Enough light makes it into the cab to tell that his head is down, his shoulders shuddering hard.

I desperately want to run outside and close myself in the truck beside him. But for the first time since I met him, I don't trust my instincts. When I hear his truck drive off, I replay everything that happened leading up to this moment.

Then I pull myself together and get up. I head out to the lot, forcing myself to be anywhere but stuck in my mind. I help several families, and I know my happiness comes across as an act, but I'm trying. Eventually, though, I can't try any longer and I go back to the trailer.

On my phone are two voice mail messages. The first is from Heather.

"Devon gave me my perfect day!" she says, almost too cheerful to handle right now. "And it isn't even Christmas! He took me to the top of Cardinals Peak for dinner, can you believe it? He was listening!"

I want to be excited for her. She deserves that. Instead, I feel jealous for how easy things can be for them.

"By the way," she says, "your trees are doing great up there. We checked."

I send her a text: I'm glad you're keeping Devon a while longer.

She texts back: He earned his way to New Year's. But he has to stop the fantasy football talk if he wants to make it to Super Bowl Sunday. How was dinner?

I don't respond.

When I start playing a voice mail from Caleb, there's a long pause before anything is spoken. "I'm sorry," he says. There's an even longer pause, and the silence is full of pain. He's been hurting a long time. "Please forgive me. I screwed that up in a way I never expected. You are worth it, Sierra. Will you allow me to stop by on my way to church tomorrow?" I hold the phone tight to my ear, listening through another pause. "I'll call you in the morning."

There are so many reasons the next week won't be easy for us. It's likely to feel worse each day we get closer to Christmas—to me leaving.

I send him a text: No need to call. Just come by.

CHAPTER SEVENTEEN

There's a knock on our trailer door the next morning. I open it as Caleb's about to knock again; his other hand holds out a to-go coffee cup with a lid to me. It's a sweet gesture from a guy whose eyes look so sad and whose hair isn't combed.

Instead of hello, he says, "I was awful."

I step down to his level and accept the drink. "You weren't awful," I say. "Maybe a little rude to Abby and your mom . . ."

"I know," he says. "And when I got home, Abby and I had a long talk. You were right. She's more okay with everything than I am. We talked about our mom and how we might be able to make this easier for her, too."

I take a first sip of the peppermint mocha.

He steps closer. "After she and I spoke, I stayed up the rest of the night thinking. My problem isn't about working things out with Abby anymore, or with my mom."

"It's about you," I say.

"I got no sleep last night thinking about that," he says.

"Judging by the look of your hair, I believe you," I say.

"At least I changed my shirt."

I look him up and down. The jeans are wrinkled but the maroon long-sleeve button-down is working for me. "I can't take the whole morning off," I say, "but can I walk with you to church?"

His church isn't far, but it's a gentle rise most of the way. The remaining heaviness from last night dissolves further with each corner we turn. We hold hands the entire time to keep us close while we talk. Every so often he rubs his thumb up and down over mine, and I do it right back.

"We went to church a few times when I was little," I say. "Mostly with my grandparents for the holidays. But my mom went all the time growing up."

"I try to make it every week," he says. "Slowly, my mom's been coming back, too."

"So you'll sometimes go by yourself?" I ask. "Were you offended when I said I don't?"

He laughs. "Maybe if you said you went all the time because you thought it made you look good. I might consider *that* offensive."

I've never had a conversation about church with my friends. It feels like it should be uncomfortable with someone I like so much, and who I want to like me, but it's not.

"So you're a believer," I say. "Have you always been?"

"I guess so. I've always had a lot of questions, though,

which some people are afraid to admit. But it gives me something to think about at night. Something other than this girl I'm hung up on."

I smile at him. "That's a very honest answer."

We turn up a side street and that's when I see the white-steepled church. The sight of it feels like I'm being allowed to glimpse such a personal side of him. This guy I met a few weeks ago comes here every Sunday, and now I'm walking there with him, holding his hand.

We stop to let a car pull into the parking lot, which is filling up fast. A few middle-aged men in orange reflective vests guide cars to the remaining open spaces. Caleb and I walk toward two etched glass doors with a large wooden cross above them. A line of several men and women, young and old, stand outside the doors greeting people as they enter the lobby. Standing to the side, probably waiting for Caleb to arrive, are his mom and Abby.

"Sierra!" Abby bounces over. "I am so relieved to see you. I was afraid my bone-headed brother scared you away last night."

Caleb throws her a sarcastic grin.

"He brought me a peppermint mocha," I say. "It's hard to say no to that."

One of the greeters behind them checks his phone and soon they're heading in, closing the glass doors behind them.

"Looks like it's time to go in," Caleb's mom says.

"Actually," Caleb says, "Sierra has to head back."

"I wish I didn't have to," I say. "But Sundays get busy, especially the week before Christmas."

Caleb's mom points a finger at him. "Something I almost forgot. Do you think you can disappear this afternoon?"

Caleb looks at me, confused, and then back to his mom.

"I'm getting a delivery and I'm trying to keep it a secret from you. And this year, I'm determined to not let you spoil it." She turns to me. "When he was little I had to keep his presents at work because he sniffed out every hiding place at home."

"That's horrible!" I say. "My parents could keep mine in their bedroom and I'd do everything to not go in there. Why would I want to accidentally see what I'm getting?"

Caleb ignores my innocence and challenges his mom. "You really don't think I can sniff out this delivery?"

"Honey . . ." She pats his arm. "That's why I said it in front of Sierra. I'm hoping she can teach you to value anticipation."

Oh, I've been anticipating a lot with this boy. "I'm watching you," I say to Caleb.

"Figure out something to do until dinner," his mom says.

Caleb looks at his sister. "Apparently I'm supposed to disappear this afternoon. What should we do, Abby-girl?"

"Figure it out now or later," their mom says, "but I'm going inside. I don't want to sit in the balcony like last time." She gives me a hug and then walks inside the church.

Abby tells Caleb to get me a flyer for the candlelight Christmas Eve service. She says, "You should definitely come with us. It's so beautiful."

Caleb asks me to wait right here, and I watch him jog toward the glass doors.

Abby looks me directly in the eyes. "My brother likes you," she says quickly. "Like, *really* likes you."

My entire body tingles.

"I know you're not here much longer," she continues, "so I wanted you to know that in case he's being a total guy with his feelings."

I don't know how to respond, and Abby laughs at my silence.

Caleb walks out holding a red flyer. He offers it to me but it takes a moment to stop staring at his eyes. On the printed side is a drawing of a lit candle surrounded by a wreath and information about the service.

"Time to go in," Abby says. She loops her arm through Caleb's and then the two of them head inside.

Yes, I say to myself, *I like your brother, too. Like,* really *like him*.

CHAPTER EIGHTEEN

Monday morning, I call Elizabeth to ask how Rachel's show went.

"She did fine," Elizabeth says. "You should really be asking her, though."

"I tried!" I say. "I called; I texted. You guys are giving me the cold shoulder."

"Because you chose a guy over her, Sierra. We get that you like him. Great. But honestly, you're not going to be down there forever," she says. "So yes, Rachel's upset with you. But she also doesn't want to see you get your heart broken."

I close my eyes as I listen. Even when they're mad at me, they still care. I groan, flopping onto my tiny bed. "It's ridiculous. It is. It's a relationship that can't go anywhere. We haven't even kissed yet!"

"Sierra, it's Christmastime. Put a stupid mistletoe over his head and kiss him already!"

"Will you do me a favor?" I ask. "Can you stop by my house? On my dresser is the cutting from my first Christmas tree. Will you mail that to me?"

Elizabeth sighs.

"I just want to show it to him," I say. "He's such a traditionalist, I think he'd love to see it before I . . ."

I stop myself. If I say it, I'll obsess over it for the rest of the day.

"Before you leave," Elizabeth finishes. "It's going to happen, Sierra."

"I know. Feel free to tell me I'm being stupid."

She doesn't respond for a long time. "It's your heart. No one else gets a say in that."

Sometimes it feels like it's not even up to the person holding the heart.

"You should probably kiss him, though, before you make any bigger decisions," she says. "If he's horrible, it'll be so much easier to let him go."

I laugh. "I miss you both so much."

"We miss you, too, Sierra. We both do. I'll try to smooth things over with Rachel. She's just frustrated."

I fall back onto my bed. "I'm a traitor to the girl code."

"Don't beat yourself up," Elizabeth says. "It's fine. We're just being selfish about sharing you, is all."

Before starting work, I sit at my laptop and video-record myself describing—in French—everything that's happened since I left home, from planting my tree on Cardinals Peak to walking Caleb to church. I send the video to Monsieur Cappeau to make up for all the phone calls I've missed.

I grab an apple and head to the Bigtop to help Mom. It's winter break for most of the schools now, and because the tree procrastinators are running out of time, the lot should be busy all day. In previous years I worked ten-hour days this week, but Mom tells me they hired a few extra students to help so I'd have more time for myself.

Working side by side with her, we restock supplies when not helping customers. Dad wheels in two more trees sprayed with fake snow. In a break between customers, all three of us huddle around the drink station. I mix myself a cheap peppermint mocha and tell them I'm making more cookies to go with Caleb's next few trees.

"That's great, honey," Dad says, but instead of looking at me, he looks outside the Bigtop. "I need to go check on the workers."

Mom and I watch him leave.

"I guess that's better than putting his foot down," I say. Dad has taken the wait-it-out approach to my relationship with Caleb. On the upside, after witnessing my confrontation with Andrew, Dad asked him to apologize to me. Rather than do that, he quit.

Mom clinks her mug against mine. "Maybe Caleb will

save some of his tips and buy a Christmas gift for you, too."

When Mom sips her coffee, I tell her, "I'm thinking about giving him the cutting from my first tree."

Her silence is deafening, so I raise my Easter mug to my lips as I wait. Outside the Bigtop, I see Luis carry a tree out to the car lot. I take another sip, wondering why he's here if he already has a tree.

When I look back, Mom says, "That's a perfect gift for someone like Caleb."

I put down my mug and hug her while she tries to keep from spilling her drink on us. "Thank you for not being weird about him, Mom."

"I trust your judgment." She puts down her mug and holds my shoulders, looking me in the eyes. "Your father does, too. I think he just decided to hold his breath until we leave again."

Over her shoulder, I see Luis walk back into the lot with work gloves on. I point him out to Mom. "That's Luis," I say. "I know him."

"He's one of the students we hired. Your dad said he's a good worker."

At the next break between customers, I warm up the mocha with some regular coffee. A voice behind me says, "Want to make me one while you're at it?"

"That depends." I turn toward Caleb. "What are you going to do for me?"

He reaches into his jacket pocket and draws out a green knit Christmas tree hat with felt ornaments and a puffy yellow star. He pulls it tight onto his head. "I was going to save this for later, but if a mocha's at stake, I'll put it on now."

"Why?" I ask, laughing.

"I bought it at a secondhand store this morning," he says. "I'm in the full sartorial spirit of the season."

My mouth drops open. "*I* don't even know what that means."

He dimple-grins and raises one eyebrow. "*Sartorial?* I'm shocked. Maybe you should put a vocab app on your phone like me. There's a new word every day and you give yourself points each time you use it."

"But did you use it correctly?" I ask.

"I think so," he says. "It's an adjective. Something about clothing."

I shake my head, wanting to both laugh and snatch that horrible thing off him. "Mister, *sartorial* just earned you double candy canes."

Caleb offers to help bake the cookies at his house, and Mom tells us to go have fun. Actually, she says I should go have fun without asking Dad, which is motherly advice I'll take.

"Abby says she would love to join us," Caleb says when we get in his truck. "You can invite Heather, too."

"Heather, believe it or not, is frantically putting together a gift for Devon," I say. "My guess is it'll be a Christmas sweater."

Caleb opens his mouth in mock-horror. "Would she do that?"

"She totally would," I say. "She'll also get him something good, but if I know Heather, she'll give him the sweater first to see how he reacts."

After we shop for ingredients, Caleb ushers me into his house, each of us carrying a bag of groceries. Abby is on the couch tapping rapidly on her phone.

Without looking up, she says, "I'll join you in a minute. I have to make sure my friends don't think I fell off the earth. And take off that ridiculous hat, Caleb."

Caleb sets his knit hat on the kitchen table. He's already set out cookie sheets, measuring spoons, cups, and a ceramic mixing bowl. "Will you send me messages like that from Oregon," he says, "so I know you haven't fallen off the earth?"

My laugh comes out sounding forced, which it is. In less than a week I need to figure out how to say goodbye.

I pull items from the grocery bags and set them on the counter.

The doorbell rings and Caleb shouts into the other room, "Are you expecting someone?"

Abby doesn't answer, probably still texting. Caleb rolls his eyes and leaves to answer the door. I hear it open, and then a pause.

Finally, Caleb says, "Hey. What are you doing here?"

The next voice—familiar and deep—reaches me all the way from the front door to the kitchen. "That the way you talk to your onetime best friend?"

I nearly drop a dozen eggs. I have no idea what Jeremiah's doing here, but I feel like running a victory lap around the kitchen, arms in the air.

Both guys walk in and I put on my calm face. "Hey, Jeremiah."

"Tree lot girl," he says.

"You know, I do other things, too."

"Trust me, I know," he says. "If it weren't for you pushing and prying, I probably wouldn't be here."

Caleb smiles and glances between the two of us. I never told him about Jeremiah and Cassandra visiting the lot.

"Now, things still aren't perfect," Jeremiah says, "but I took a stand with Cassandra and my mom, and . . . I'm here."

Caleb turns to me, his eyes full of questions and unspoken gratitude. He rubs his forehead and turns to look out the kitchen window.

I start putting the ingredients back in the bags. This moment is not about me, and it shouldn't be. "You guys talk. I'm going to bring these to Heather's."

Still facing the window, Caleb starts to tell me I don't have to leave, but I stop him.

"Talk to your friend," I say, not even trying to hide my smile. "It's been a while."

When I turn around, grocery bags packed, Caleb's looking at me with pure love.

"Let's meet up later," I say.

"Is seven o'clock good?" he asks. "There's something I want you to see."

I smile. "I'm looking forward to it."

When I reach the front door, I hear Jeremiah say, "I missed you, man."

My heart swells and I take a breath before opening the door.

🌲

After we drop off our latest tree along with a tin of Christmas cookies, Caleb and I drive around while he updates me on his reunion with Jeremiah.

"It's hard to say when we'll hang out next," Caleb says, "because he's got his friends now, and I've got mine. But we will, which is sort of amazing. I assumed we never would again."

"That *is* amazing," I say.

We park in front of Caleb's house and he turns to me. "It's because of you," he says. "*You're* amazing."

I want this moment to last, the two of us in his truck feeling grateful for each other. Instead, he opens his door, letting in the cool air.

"Come on," he says, and then he steps out.

He walks around to the sidewalk and I shake the nerves from my fingers before opening my door. When I get out, I rub my hands to warm them, and then he takes my hand and we go for a walk.

He leads me past four of his neighbors' houses and around the corner to an alleyway. The entrance to the alley is lit by a single lamppost. The ground is rough asphalt with a smooth concrete gulley running down the middle.

"We call this Garage Alley," he says.

The further we move into the alley, the more the light from the lamppost fades. On either side, short driveways lead to garages. High wooden fences around the backyards keep out most light from the houses. I almost lose my balance in the gulley, but Caleb grabs my arm.

"It's kind of spooky back here," I say.

"I hope you're ready," he says, "because I am about to majorly disappoint you." He tries to make his shadowy face look serious, but I can see a slight grin.

We stop where the alley meets his driveway, and he turns my shoulders toward the garage. The large metal door is mostly buried in the shadow of the roof's overhang. He takes my hand and pulls me forward. A motion sensor above the door clicks on an attached light.

"My mom warned you that I'm terrible with surprises," he says.

I push his shoulder. "You did not!"

He laughs. "Not on purpose! Not this time. I had to get bungee cords out of the garage, and my present was right there."

"You ruined your mom's surprise?"

"It was her fault!" he says. "It was right there! But I think you'll be glad because now I can share it with you. So you won't tell her, right?"

I can't believe this. He is acting like such a little kid, which is far too cute to be annoying. "Just show me what it is," I say.

CHAPTER NINETEEN

The motion sensor light stays on, and Caleb walks to a control box mounted beside the garage door. He lifts a hinged plastic flap, which covers a pushbutton keypad.

"When we were little," he says, his finger hovering over the first number, "every year I asked Santa for the same gift. A few of my friends had one and I was so jealous, but I never got one. After a while I gave up and stopped asking, and I guess everyone assumed I outgrew it. But I totally didn't."

His smile is radiant.

"Show it to me!" I say.

Caleb's fingers tap-dance a four-digit code and then he closes the flap. He steps back and the garage door slowly rolls open. I'm pretty sure he didn't ask for a convertible as a child, though that would make tonight very fun. When the door is halfway up, I duck to peek inside. Enough light creeps in that I can see . . . *a trampoline*? I collapse onto my knees laughing.

"Why is that funny?" Caleb says. "Jumping is fun!"

I look up at him, but he knows exactly why it's hysterical. "Did you just say that? 'Jumping is fun'? How old are you?"

"Mature enough not to care," he says. When the door is all the way up, he enters the garage. "Come on."

I look at the low wooden beams of the ceiling. "We can't jump in there," I say.

"Of course not. How old are *you*?" He grips one side of the trampoline and bends his knees. "Help me out."

A few feet at a time, we carry the trampoline onto the driveway.

"Aren't you worried your mom will hear?" I ask. For me, the giddiness on his face makes that possibility worth it. So much for teaching him the value of anticipation.

"It's the holiday office party," he says. "She won't be home until late."

"And Abby?"

"She went to a movie with a friend." He steps on the heels of his shoes to pop them off and then springs onto the trampoline. Before I get my first shoe off he's already leaping about like a goofy gazelle. "Stop stalling and get up here."

I slip off my second shoe, lift myself onto the edge, and then swing my socked feet around. It only takes a few minutes and we develop a rhythm as we circle and laugh around each other. One goes up as the other comes down. He keeps bouncing higher to give me more spring and soon we're catching enough air for Caleb to get fancy and do a backflip.

It's amazing to see him so free and unburdened. Not that he's always serious, but this feels different, like he's recapturing something he lost.

Despite his pleading, I refuse to attempt a flip, and eventually we both get tired enough to take a break. We plop down onto our backs. The night sky is brilliant with stars. We're both breathing heavily, with only our chests moving up and down, slower and slower. After a minute of near stillness, the light on the garage flicks off.

"Look at those stars," Caleb says.

The driveway is dark and the night is so quiet. I can only hear our breathing, a few soft crickets in the ivy, and a bird in a distant neighbor's tree. Then, from Caleb's side, I hear a metal spring squeak.

Keeping still so the light stays off, I ask, "What are you doing?"

"Moving very, very slowly," he says. "I want to hold your hand in the dark."

I move my head as little and as slowly as possible to look down at my hand. Our silhouettes are dark against the even darker stretch of trampoline. His fingers sneak closer to mine. Still needing to catch my breath, I wait for his touch.

A blue spark shoots between us. I jerk to the side. *"Ow!"*

The light kicks on and Caleb laughs hysterically. "I am so sorry!"

"You'd better be sorry," I say. "That wasn't romantic at all!"

"You can shock me back," he says. "That's romantic, right?"

Still on my back, I rub my feet back and forth hard against the trampoline, and then I reach over to his earlobe. *Pzzt!*

"Ah!" He grabs his ear, laughing. "That actually hurt!"

He pushes himself to his feet and then shuffles his socks across the surface of the trampoline in one big circle. I stand up and mirror his movements as we stare at each other.

"What, are we doing battle here?" I ask. "Bring it."

"You bet we are." He points a finger in front of him and lunges for me.

I duck to the side and zap his shoulder. "Twice! I got you twice."

"All right, no more Mr. Nice Guy."

I skip-jog to the other side of the trampoline, but he's right behind me, his fingers reaching out. Watching his feet closely, I do a small hop to land just as he steps, fully knocking him off balance. He falls forward and I shock the back of his neck.

I throw my hands in the air. "Denied!"

Laid out, he looks up at me with an evil sneer. I glance around but there's no escape on a trampoline. He does a quick hop to his knees and then his feet and tackles me. We bounce once and he twists so that I drop on top of him. The breath rushes out of me. His hands clasp behind my back, holding me tight. I raise my head enough to see his eyes, blow my hair out of his face, and we both laugh. Slowly, the laughing stops, our chests and stomachs breathing hard against each other.

He touches my cheek with his hand and guides me toward him. His lips are so soft against mine, sweetened with peppermint. I lean farther in and get lost kissing him. I slide off him to the mat and then he rolls himself on top of me. I wrap my arms around him and we kiss with more intensity. We pull back to catch our breaths and look into each other's eyes.

There are so many things prickling in the back of my mind, threatening to take me out of this moment. But instead of worrying about anything, I close my eyes, lean forward, and allow myself to believe in us.

The drive back to the lot is mostly quiet. I find myself nearly hypnotized by Caleb's keychain, swaying with our picture on Santa's lap. If only this week would never end.

When he pulls into the lot and parks, he takes my hand. I look to the trailer, and a curtain in Mom and Dad's room swings shut.

Caleb holds my hand tighter. "Thank you, Sierra."

"For what?"

He smiles. "For bouncing on the trampoline with me."

"Oh, my pleasure," I say.

"And for making these past few weeks the best I've ever had."

He leans over to kiss me, and once again I lose myself in his kiss. I trace my lips from his jaw to his ear and whisper, "Mine too."

Pressing our cheeks together, listening to each other breathe, we don't move. After next week, it will never be like this again. I want to hold this moment and imprint it on my heart so it never fades.

When I finally get out of the truck, I watch the taillights of his truck until they have long disappeared.

Dad walks up behind me. "That has to be the end, Sierra. I don't want you seeing him anymore."

I spin toward him.

He shakes his head. "It's not the thing with his sister. Not just that. It's everything."

The warm and beautiful feeling I've experienced all evening bleeds out of me, replaced by a heavy dread. "I thought you were letting it go."

"We're leaving soon," he says, "you know that. And you must know that you've been growing way too attached."

I can't find my voice or even the words to shout at him. Things were finally going right and he has to ruin that? No. I will not let him do this.

"What does Mom say?" I ask.

He turns slightly toward the trailer. "She doesn't want you to get hurt, either." When I don't respond, he turns the rest of the way and begins to walk back to the cramped trailer that used to feel like home.

I turn toward the Christmas trees. Behind me, I can hear Dad's boots shuffle up the metal steps and the door closing behind him. I can't go in there. Not yet. So I walk into the trees, the needles scratching against my sleeves and pants. I sit down in the cool dirt where the outside lights can't reach me.

I try to imagine myself back home, where these trees around me once grew, looking up at these same stars.

Back in the trailer, I barely sleep all night. When I first pulled open my curtains, the sun still hadn't risen. I lay on my bed, looking out, watching the stars slowly begin to fade. The more they disappeared, the more lost I felt.

I decide to reach out to Rachel. We haven't spoken since I missed her performance, but she knows me better than anyone, and I just need to tell her how I feel. I send her an apology text. I tell her I miss her. I tell her she would love Caleb but that my parents think I'm getting too close to him.

Eventually, she responds: **Can I help?**

I let out a deep breath and close my eyes, just so grateful to have Rachel in my life.

I tell her: **I need a Christmas miracle.**

In the long pause that follows, I watch the sun start to rise.

She answers: **Give me two days.**

Caleb shows up the next day with a big grin, carrying a package wrapped in Sunday comics and way too much tape. Behind him I can see Mom watching us. While visibly not thrilled, she stays with her customer.

"What's that?" I ask, swallowing my fear of Dad returning from his lunch run. "I mean, besides an invitation to teach you how to wrap."

He hands it to me. "There's only one way to find out."

The gift is somewhat floppy, and when I tear into the package I see why. It's that silly knitted Christmas tree hat he wore the other day. "No, I think this belongs to you."

"I know, but I saw how envious you were," he says, unable to hide his smile. "I figured, your winters get much colder than ours."

I bet he doesn't think I'll wear it, which is why I put it on immediately.

He pulls the sides down over my ears, and then leaves his hands there as he bends forward to kiss me. I let the kiss happen, but I keep my lips tight. When he doesn't pull back, I have to.

"I'm sorry," he says. "I shouldn't do that here."

A throat clears behind him and I look over his shoulder.

"I need you to get back to work, Sierra," Mom says.

Caleb, clearly embarrassed, looks out at the trees. "Am I about to get outhouse duty?"

Nobody laughs.

He looks at me. "What's going on?"

I look down and see Mom's shoes move closer.

"Caleb," she says, "Sierra has told us wonderful things about you."

I look up at her, my eyes begging her to be gentle.

"And I know how she feels about you," Mom says. She looks at me but doesn't even attempt to smile. "But we're leaving in a week and, more than likely, we won't be back next year."

I don't take my eyes away from hers, but I can see Caleb turn to me, and my heart breaks. That was for me to tell him *if* necessary, and because nothing is certain it was not necessary yet.

"Her father and I aren't comfortable seeing this relationship progress without everyone knowing where we stand." She looks at me. "Your dad will be back in a minute. Let's wrap this up."

She leaves and I'm left alone with Caleb, his face a mix of betrayal and surrender.

"Is your dad not supposed to see me?" he asks.

"He thinks we're getting too serious," I say. "You don't have to be afraid, he's just feeling overprotective."

"Overprotective because you're not coming back?"

"That's still not for sure," I say. I can't look him in the eyes anymore. "I should have told you."

"Well, now's your chance," he says. "What else aren't you telling me?"

A tear falls from my cheek. I didn't even know I was crying, but I don't care if I am. "Andrew talked to him," I say, "but it's okay."

His voice is rigid. "How is that okay?"

"Because then I talked to them and I told them—"

"Told them what? Because we're talking right now and everything is definitely not okay."

I look at him and wipe the tears from my cheeks. "Caleb . . ."

"This is not going to change, Sierra. Not in whatever time your family has left. So why are you bothering with me?"

I reach for his hand. "Caleb . . ."

He steps back, forcing distance between us.

"Don't," I whisper.

"I said you were worth it, Sierra, and you are. But I don't know if the rest of this is. And I know I'm not."

"Yes," I say, "Caleb, you—"

He turns and leaves the Bigtop, then walks straight to his truck and drives away.

The next day, Dad returns from the post office and drops a thick express envelope next to me at the register. Twenty-four hours have passed without Dad and me speaking. We've never been like this, but I can't forgive him. At the top of the envelope is a red heart drawn around *Elizabeth Campbell* in the return address. After getting through two more customers I tear open the package.

Inside are a letter-size envelope and a glittery red box the size of a hockey puck. I take the top off the box, remove a square of cotton, and there's the inch-thick cutting from my first tree. Around the edge it retains a thin layer of rough bark. In the center is the Christmas tree I painted on it when I was eleven years old. Two days ago, looking at this would have made me nervous about how Caleb would react if I gave it to him. Now, I don't feel anything.

A customer steps up to the counter and I put the lid back

on the box. When she leaves, I open the letter. While Elizabeth sent me the tree cutting, the note is in Rachel's handwriting: *I hope this helps with that Christmas miracle you asked for.*

Along with the note are two tickets to the winter formal. *Snow Globe of Love* is written in fancy red script across the top. On the left side is a couple dancing within a snow globe as silver glitter falls around them.

I close my eyes.

CHAPTER TWENTY

On my lunch break I go to the trailer and hide the red box beneath a pillow on my bed. I remove the picture of Caleb and me tucked against the window seam and slip the tickets between the photo and the cardboard backing.

Before I lose my courage, I find Dad and ask him to take another walk with me. I've been stewing about this long enough. I help him strap a tree to a customer's car and then we walk away from the lot together.

"I need you to reconsider this," I tell him. "You say it's not all about Caleb's past, and I believe you."

"Good, because—"

I interrupt him. "You said it's also because we have less than a week left and I'm falling for him. And you're right, I am," I say. "I know that makes you uncomfortable for a million reasons, but I also know you wouldn't say anything about it if you couldn't use his past as an excuse."

"I don't know, maybe, but I still—"

"And while that makes me so mad because it's not fair to Caleb, you're forgetting about the one person who should be the most important part of this for you."

"Sierra, you're all I'm thinking about here," he says. "Yes, it's hard watching my baby girl fall in love. And yes, it's hard to block out his past. But more than anything, honey, I can't stand by and watch you get your heart broken."

"Shouldn't that be my decision?" I say.

"Yes, if you can take everything into account." He stops walking and looks out to the street. "Your mother and I haven't said this to each other yet, but we both know it. It's almost certain we're not coming back next year."

I touch his arm. "I am so sorry, Dad."

Still facing the street, he puts an arm around me, and I lean my head against his chest. "Me too," he says.

"So you're mostly worried about how I'm going to feel leaving," I say.

He looks down at me, and I know I am the most important part of this to him. "You can't understand how hard that will be," he says.

"Then tell me," I say. "Because you know. What did you feel when you first met Mom and then had to leave?"

"It was awful," he says. "A couple of times I thought we weren't going to make it. We even took a break and dated other people for a while. That damn near killed me."

My next question is what I've been building to. "And was it worth it?"

He smiles at me and then turns to look back at our lot. "Of course it was."

"Well then," I say.

"Sierra, your mom and I had both been in serious relationships before. This is your first time being in love."

"I never said I was in love!"

He laughs. "You don't have to say it."

We both look out at the cars, and I pull his arm tighter around me.

He looks down at me and sighs. "Your heart is going to break in a few days," he says. "It will. But I won't make it hurt more by taking away the next few days with him."

I hug both of my arms around him and tell him that I love him.

"I know," he whispers back. "And you know that your mom and I will be here to help put your heart back together."

With his arm around my shoulder, and my arm hugging his side, we walk back to the lot.

"I need you to consider one thing," he says. "Think about how this season will end for the two of you. Because it will. So don't ignore it."

When he joins Mom in the Bigtop, I run to the trailer and call Caleb.

"Get over here and buy a tree," I say. "I know you have deliveries to make."

It's dark by the time I see Caleb pull into the parking area. Luis and I carry a big, heavy tree toward his truck.

"I hope this fits wherever you're going," Luis says.

Caleb hops out and runs back to lower the tailgate. "That one might be out of my price range," he says, "even with a discount."

"No," I say, "because it's free."

"It's a gift from her parents," Luis says. "They're taking a nap at the moment, so—"

"I'm right here, Luis," I say. "I can tell him."

Luis blushes and then heads back to the lot, where a customer waits to have her tree netted. Caleb, meanwhile, looks confused.

"My dad and I had a talk," I say.

"And?"

"And they trust me," I tell him. "They also love what you do with their trees, so they want to donate this one to the cause."

He looks toward the trailer and a faint smile appears. "I guess when we get back you can let them know whether their donation fit."

After we deliver the tree, which barely fits—and the five-year-old *freaks* with excitement—Caleb drives us to Cardinals Peak. He parks in front of the metal gate and unlocks his door.

"Wait here and I'll open it up," he says. "We can drive to the top and, if you don't mind, I'd love to finally see your trees."

"Then turn off the engine," I say. "We're hiking up."

He leans forward to look up the hill.

"What, are you afraid of a little night hike?" I tease. "I'm sure you have a flashlight, right? Please don't tell me you drive a truck but don't have a flashlight!"

"Yes," he says, "in fact, I do have one of those."

"Perfect."

He backs his truck onto a grass-and-dirt patch on the side of the street and grabs a flashlight from the glove box. "There's only one," he says. "I hope you're okay standing close."

"Oh, if we must," I say.

He hops out of the truck, walks over to my side, and opens the door. We both zip up our jackets while looking at the tall silhouette of Cardinals Peak.

"I love coming out here," I say. "Every time I hike up this hill, I think . . . I get this feeling like . . . that my trees are a deep personal metaphor."

"Wow," Caleb says. "That might be the most profound thing I've heard you say yet."

"Oh, shut it," I say. "Give me that flashlight."

He hands me the light but keeps on going. "Seriously. Do you mind if I use that at school? My English teacher will love it."

I nudge him with my shoulder. "Hey, I was raised on a Christmas tree farm. I'm allowed to get sentimental about it even if I can't express myself."

I love how Caleb and I can tease each other and it feels like no big deal. The hard things are still there—we can't avoid a day on the calendar—but we have found a way to appreciate each other right now.

It's colder tonight than when Heather and I came here on Thanksgiving. Caleb and I don't say much on the way up; we simply enjoy the coolness in the air and the warmth of our touch. Before the final turn of the hill, I lead him off the road with the flashlight and into knee-high brush. Without complaint, he follows me out several yards.

The crescent moon casts deep shadows on this side of the hill. Where the brush clears, I slowly move the flashlight across my trees, capturing one or two at a time within the narrow beam.

Caleb steps beside me and puts an arm around my shoulders, gently bringing our bodies together. When I look at him, he's looking out at the trees. He lets go of me and walks into my little farm, looking so happy as he glances between them and me.

"They're beautiful," he says. He leans close and breathes in one of the trees. "Just like Christmas."

"And they look like Christmas because Heather hikes up every summer to shear them," I say.

"They don't grow wild like this?"

"Not all of them," I say. "Dad likes to tell people we all need a little help getting in the spirit."

"Your family likes metaphors," Caleb says. He walks behind me and wraps me in a hug, letting his chin rest on my shoulder.

We quietly look at the trees together for several minutes.

"I love them," he tells me. "They're your little tree family."

I lean to the side and look him in the eyes. "Now who's being sentimental?"

"Have you ever thought of decorating them?" he asks.

"Heather and I did that once—in the most eco-friendly way possible, of course. We used pinecones and berries and flowers, plus some stars we bought made of birdseed and honey."

"You brought gifts for the birdies?" he says. "Very cute."

We climb back through the brush, and I turn around to admire my trees once more—probably the last time I'll see them before I leave. I hold Caleb's hand, not knowing how many more chances I'll get to do this in my life. He points away, toward my family's tree lot. From up here it looks like a small, softly lit rectangle. The lampposts and snowflakes that link between the trees brighten their deep green. There's the Bigtop and the silver trailer. I can see bodies move between the trees, a mix of customers, workers, and maybe Mom and Dad. Caleb slides behind me again and wraps me in his arms.

This is home, I think. *Down there . . . and right here.*

He runs his hand down my arm that holds the flashlight, and then moves the beam of light slowly across my trees. "I'm counting five," he says. "I thought you said there were six."

My heart stops. I move the flashlight back across my trees. "One, two . . ." My heart shatters when I stop at five. I run back through the brush, sweeping the beam rapidly back and forth along the ground ahead of me. "It's the first one! The big one."

Caleb walks toward me through brush. Before he reaches me, he knocks his foot against something solid. I shine the light at his feet and then clasp a hand over my mouth. I kneel onto the soil beside the stump, which is all that remains of my oldest tree. At the top of the cut are small beads of dried sap.

Caleb kneels beside me. He takes the flashlight from me and holds both of my hands. "Someone fell in love with it," he says. "It's probably in their home now, all decorated and beautiful. It's like a gift that—"

"It was a gift for *me* to give," I say. "Not for someone to take."

He eases me to my feet and I rest my cheek against his shoulder. After several minutes like this, we begin our walk back down the road. We walk slowly and say nothing. He gently guides me around any holes and rocks.

Then he stops, peering a few feet off the side of the road. I follow his gaze as he steps toward it. The flashlight illuminates the dark green of my tree, tossed on its side and left drying in the brush.

"They just left it here?" I say.

"I guess your tree put up a fight."

I slump down and don't bother holding back my tears. "I hate whoever did this!"

Caleb moves next to me and rests a hand on my back. He doesn't say anything, doesn't tell me it'll be all right or judge me for how worked up I am over a tree. He simply understands.

Eventually, I get up. He brushes the tears from my face and looks me in the eyes. He still doesn't speak, but I know he's with me.

"I wish I could explain why I'm acting like this," I say, but he closes his eyes and then I close mine, and I know I don't need to.

I look at the tree again. Whoever saw it up there, they thought it looked so beautiful. They thought they could make it more beautiful. And they tried, they really wanted it, but it was too much for them.

So they left it.

"I don't want to be here," I say.

Caleb walks behind me, aiming the light at my feet as I lead us away.

🌲

When Heather calls to see if she can hang out at the lot, I tell her about the tree on Cardinals Peak and that I may not be the best company. Because she knows me well, she comes right over. She tells me I've been a "tree-delivering ghost" this year and she's sad we haven't spent as much time together. I remind her that whenever I've had an hour or two free, she's been with Devon.

"So much for Operation Ditch the Boyfriend," I say.

Heather helps me restock the drink station. "I suppose I never really wanted to ditch him, I just wanted him to be a better boyfriend. We started off so great but then he got . . . I don't know . . ."

"Complacent?"

She rolls her eyes. "Sure. We'll use one of your words."

I catch her up on all the drama with Andrew and Dad, and how it required two talks to get my parents to understand why it isn't an option to not see Caleb in the time we have left.

"Look at my girl putting her foot down," Heather says. She takes my hand and squeezes it. "I still hope you come back next year, Sierra. But if not, I'm glad this one's turning out the way it is."

"I guess so," I say. "But did it have to get so bumpy?"

"Well, now it means so much more," she says. "Take me and Devon. He got complacent, right? Every day was the same thing and so boring. I was considering breaking up with him and then that Snow Queen thing happened. It caused tension, but then he gave me my perfect day. Where we are now, we earned this. And you and Caleb definitely earned these next few days."

"I think we've earned enough for the next few years," I say. "And Caleb's earned enough for a lifetime."

An hour later, Heather leaves to work on her surprise gift for Devon. The rest of the day moves slowly with customers trickling in. I count out the register at night and put everything away that needs to be locked up.

Mom walks over as I flip the switch to turn off the snowflake lights. "Dad and I would like to take you out to dinner," she says.

We drive to Breakfast Express, and when we enter the packed train car, Caleb is filling a man's coffee a few tables away. Without looking up, he says, "Be with you in a minute."

"Take your time," Dad says, smiling.

Caleb must be exhausted. He looks straight at us for several steps before he registers who we are. At that, he laughs and then grabs a few menus.

"You look tired," I say.

"One guy called in sick so I came in early," he says. "At least that means more tips."

We follow him to an empty booth near the kitchen. After we sit, he sets down our napkins and silverware.

"I can probably buy two trees tomorrow," he says. "People are still buying trees, right? Even though it's so close to Christmas?"

"We're still open," Dad tells him. "But not as busy as you look here."

Caleb leaves to get us some waters. I watch him walk away looking a bit frantic but completely adorable. When I glance across the table, Dad's shaking his head at me.

"You're going to have to learn to ignore your father," Mom says. "That's how I put up with him."

Dad gives Mom a peck on the cheek. Twenty years in, she knows how to shut him down when he's being ridiculous, but in a way that he loves.

"Mom, did you ever want to do anything besides work on the farm?" I ask.

She gives me a quizzical look. "It's not what I went to college for, if that's what you mean."

Caleb returns with three waters and three wrapped straws. "Do you know what you'd like?"

"I am so sorry," Mom says. "We haven't even looked at our menus yet."

"Don't worry, that's actually perfect," Caleb says. "There's a *lovely* couple—I'm being sarcastic—who apparently need more of my attention."

He darts off, and Mom and Dad pick up their menus.

"But do you ever have days when you wonder?" I ask. "What would your life have been like if it didn't entirely revolve around a holiday?"

Mom puts her menu down and studies me. "Do you regret this, Sierra?"

"No," I say, "but it's all I've known. You at least had some normal Christmases before you got married. You have something to compare it to."

"I have never regretted the life I chose," Mom says. "And it was my choice, so I can be proud of that. I chose this life with your dad."

"It's been an interesting life, that's for sure," Dad says.

I pretend to read the menu. "It's been an interesting year."

"And there are only a few days left," Mom says. When I glance up, she's looking sorrowfully at Dad.

The next afternoon, Caleb's truck pulls up to the lot with Jeremiah in the passenger seat. The way they get out laughing and talking, they look like two guys who've never had a painful gap in their friendship.

Luis walks up to them and takes off a work glove to shake their hands. They all chat briefly before Caleb and Jeremiah head to the Bigtop.

"Lot girl!" Jeremiah says, offering me a fist bump. "My boy says you may need extra help pulling this place down on Christmas. Where do I sign up?"

"Won't you have plans with your family?" I ask.

"We do all our presents Christmas Eve before mass," he says. "Then we sleep in and watch football all day. But I kind of owe you one, you know?"

I look between the two of them. "So everything's okay here?"

Jeremiah looks down. "My parents don't exactly know where I am right now. Cassandra's covering for me."

"She's covering on one condition," Caleb says. He looks at me. "On New Year's Eve this guy's the designated driver for the entire cheer squad."

Jeremiah laughs. "It's a tough job, but I'm up for it." He starts walking backward away from us. "I'm going to find your dad to ask about teardown."

"What about you?" I say to Caleb. "Are you going to help us tear the place down?"

"I'd spend the day here if I could," he says, "but we have traditions I wouldn't feel good about leaving. You can understand, right?"

"Of course. And I'm glad you can all be together," I say.

Even though I mean it, I won't be glad to see Christmas morning come. "If you can find any time to duck out, I'll be at Heather's for a little while, exchanging gifts with her and Devon."

He smiles, but his eyes mirror the same sadness I feel. "I'll make it work."

While we wait for Jeremiah to return, neither one of us knows what else to say. Leaving feels so real now . . . and so soon. A couple of weeks ago it felt like this day was far away. We had time to see what could happen and how far we could fall. Now it feels like it all happened too late.

Caleb takes my hand and I follow him around to the back of the trailer, away from anyone. Before I can ask what we're doing, we're kissing. He's kissing me and I kiss him like it could be the last time. I can't stop wondering if this *is* the last time.

When he pulls back, his lips are deep red and a little swollen. Mine feel the same. He holds the side of my face and we press our foreheads together.

"I'm sorry I can't help on Christmas," he says.

"We only have a few days," I tell him. "I don't know what we're going to do."

"Come with me to the candlelight service," he says. "The one Abby told you about."

I hesitate. I haven't been to church in forever. It seems like on Christmas Eve he should be surrounded by people who believe what he believes and who feel what he feels.

His dimple returns. "I want you there. Please?"

I smile back at him. "Okay."

He starts to return to the lot, but I grab his hand and pull him back. He raises an eyebrow. "What do you need now?"

"Today's vocab word," I say. "Or are you done trying to impress me?"

"I can't believe you doubt me," he says. "Truth is, I'm really getting into these weird words. Like today's, it's *diaphanous*."

I blink. "Another one I don't know."

He raises his arms in the air. "Yes!"

"Okay, that may be the word," I say, cocking an eyebrow, "but what does it mean?"

He cocks an eyebrow right back. "It's something delicate, or translucent. Wait, you know what *translucent* means, right?"

I laugh and drag him out of hiding.

Luis waves us down and comes jogging over. "The guys and I picked out a perfect tree for you," he tells Caleb. It's been great to see Luis become part of the lot family. "We just finished putting it in your truck."

"Thanks, man," Caleb says. "Give me the tag and I'll pay for it."

Luis shakes his head. "No, we got this one."

Caleb looks at me, but I have no idea what's going on.

"Some of the baseball guys, they think it's cool what you're doing," Luis says. "And so do I. We figured we could kick in a few bucks from our tips and buy this one."

I nudge Caleb with my shoulder. His good deeds are becoming contagious.

Luis looks at me, a little nervous. "Don't worry, we didn't use the employee discount."

"Oh, you shouldn't worry about that," I say.

CHAPTER TWENTY-ONE

The day before Christmas Eve, Heather picks up Abby and brings her to the lot. Abby has been bugging Caleb to see if she can help me out because, apparently, she's wanted to work on a tree lot since she was a kid. Even if that's an exaggeration, I'm happy to indulge her.

At the far end of the Bigtop we set up two sawhorses and lay a plywood piece the size of a door across them. We pile that high with tree clippings, and the three of us stuff the trimmings into paper bags and let customers take them home. People love to decorate table settings and windowsills with these before their families come over. The bags are going almost as fast as we can fill them.

"What's this secret you got Devon for Christmas?" I ask. "My bet's on a Christmas sweater."

"Well, I did think about that," Heather says, "but I went with something better. Wait here."

She runs back to the counter to where she left her purse. Abby and I look at each other and shrug. On her way back, Heather proudly holds up a two-foot-long, slightly twisted red and green . . . scarf?

"My mom's been showing me how to knit," she says.

I bite the inside of my cheek to keep from laughing. "Christmas is in two days, Heather."

She looks at the scarf, defeated. "I had no idea it would take this long. But I figure after I leave here, I'll lock myself in my room and watch kitten videos for however many hours it takes to finish."

"If nothing else," I say, "it's the perfect way to ascertain his love."

Abby stops filling a bag. "I forget, what's *ascertain*?"

Heather and I both crack up.

"What I think it means," Heather says, stuffing the scarf in her pocket, "is if Devon really loves me, he'll wear this crappy scarf like it's the most beautiful thing he's ever received."

"That's what it means," I say, "but that's not really a fair test."

"You'd wear it if I gave it to you," Heather says, and she's right. "If he can't give me that same devotion, he doesn't deserve his real gift."

"Which is what?" Abby asks.

"Tickets to a comedy festival," she says.

"Much better," I tell her.

Heather tells Abby about the perfect day Devon gave her as an early Christmas present. One day, Abby says, she wants a boyfriend who'll carry a picnic to the top of Cardinals Peak for her.

Heather smiles while stuffing her next bag. "It's not like *he* didn't enjoy himself up there."

I throw a handful of tree trimmings at her. She does not need to expand on that with Caleb's little sister right here.

Once Abby's mom picks her up, the conversation turns to my love life. "It feels like there's so much left for us here, but I'm leaving way too soon."

"And next year's still up in the air?" she asks.

"Not very high in the air," I say. "In fact, it's highly doubtful. I don't know what I'll do if I can't see you next winter."

"It won't feel like Christmas, that's for sure," Heather says.

"My whole life, I've wondered what it would be like to stay home after Thanksgiving," I say. "To have the chance of a white Christmas and experience things normal people do over the break. But to be honest, wondering about it is not the same as wanting it."

By now, Heather and I have stopped filling bags.

"Have you discussed this with Caleb?"

"It's been hanging over us the entire time."

"What about spring break?" Heather asks. "You don't have to wait forever to see him again."

"He'll be at his dad's," I say. I think about the winter formal tickets I hid behind our picture. To give him those, I would need to know for certain where we stand. I'd have to know what we both want. It would mean leaving here, but bringing the promise of him with me.

"If Devon and I can figure it out," Heather says, "so can you and Caleb."

"I don't know if that's true," I say. "You get to be together while you do it."

🌲

After we close for the year on Christmas Eve, my parents and I have dinner in the Airstream. The roast beef has simmered in the Crock-Pot all day, so the entire trailer smells delicious. Heather's dad made and delivered corn bread. From across the tiny table, Dad asks for my thoughts concerning not coming back next year.

I break my corn bread in half. "It's out of my control," I say. "Every time we close on Christmas Eve, this is where we sit and eat. The only thing different is that question."

"That's from *your* perspective," Mom says. "From this side of the table, every year looks different."

I pull off a piece of my corn bread and slowly chew it.

"You've got a lot of people wanting the best for you," Dad says. "In here, in this town, back home . . ."

Mom leans across the table and takes my hand. "I'm sure it feels like we're all pulling you in different directions, but that's because we all care. If nothing else, I hope this year has shown you that."

Dad being Dad, he has to say, "Even if it ends up breaking your heart."

Mom nudges Dad in the shoulder. "In high school, Mr.

Cynical—your father—spent his summer at baseball camp here after meeting me the winter before."

"I got to know you very well in that time," Dad says.

"How well could you have known me in a few weeks?" Mom asks.

"Pretty well," I say. "Trust me."

Dad places his hand on top of mine and Mom's. "We're proud of you, honey. Whatever changes happen to the family business, we'll make it work as a family. And whatever you decide with Caleb, we . . . you know . . . we can . . ."

"We support you," Mom says.

"Right." Dad sits back and puts his arm around Mom. "We trust you."

I move over to their side of the table and lean into a family hug. I can feel Dad crane his neck to look at Mom.

When I return to my seat, Mom excuses herself. She goes to their room to gather the small handful of gifts we brought with us. The least patient one of us is Dad—he's a lot like Caleb that way—so he tears into his gift first.

He holds the box at arm's length. "An Elf on the Shelf?" He scrunches his nose. "Are you serious?"

Mom and I nearly die laughing. Dad complains about that toy doll every year, swearing he will never buy in to it. Since he spends December in a trailer away from home, he assumed he wouldn't have to.

"The plan was," Mom says, "Sierra and I would hide it at home when you left for California."

"And then," I say, leaning forward for maximum effect,

"you'd spend the entire month thinking about it, wondering where it was."

"That would drive me crazy," Dad says. He pulls out the elf and hangs it upside down by one foot. "You outdid yourselves this year."

"I guess if there is a silver lining," I say, "now you may get to look for it every day at home."

"There's another example," Dad says, "of not always needing a silver lining."

"Okay, my turn," Mom says.

Every year, she wants to be surprised with a different scented body lotion. While she thankfully loves the smell of Christmas trees, after being immersed in them for a month, she wants to smell like something else in the new year.

She unwraps this year's bottle and turns it around to read the label. "Cucumber licorice? How in the world did you find this?"

"It's your two favorite scents," I remind her.

She pops open the top, smells it, and then squirts a drop onto her palm. "This stuff is incredible!" she says, and she rubs it around her hands.

Dad hands me a small silver gift box.

I shimmy the box open and lift out a bit of cotton. A car key practically glistens beneath it. "You bought me a car!"

"Technically, it's Uncle Bruce's truck," Mom says, "but we'll have the insides reupholstered in whatever colors you want."

"It may not be sensible for long drives," Dad says, "but it's great for the farm and getting around town."

"Do you mind that it's his?" Mom asks. "We couldn't afford what you—"

"Thank you," I say. I turn the box over so the key falls into my hand. After feeling its weight for several seconds, I launch from my seat again and hug them both so hard. "This is incredible."

For tradition's sake, after the dirty dishes are piled into the sink, we climb into my parents' bed and watch *How the Grinch Stole Christmas* on my laptop. As usual, Mom and Dad are fast asleep by the time the Grinch's heart grows three sizes that day. I'm wide awake, my stomach in a million knots because it's now time to get ready for the candlelight service with Caleb.

Tonight there's no need to try on a bunch of outfits. Before I even move from their bed, I settle on my simple black skirt and a white blouse. In the tiny bathroom, I flatiron my hair. When I'm carefully applying makeup, I see Mom's reflection smile behind me in the mirror. She holds up a new pink cashmere sweater.

"In case it gets cold out," she says.

I spin around. "Where did you get this?"

"It was your father's idea," she says. "He wanted you to have something new for tonight."

I hold up the sweater. "Dad picked this out?"

Mom laughs. "Of course not. And thank your lucky stars,

Jay Asher

because if he did it'd probably cover more than a snowsuit," she says. "He asked me to get you something while you girls were putting trimmings in the bags."

I look in the mirror and hold the sweater up to myself. "Tell him I love it."

She smiles at our reflections. "If I can wake him up after you leave, we're going to pop some popcorn and watch *White Christmas.*"

They do that every year, usually with me cuddled between them. "I've always admired that you and Dad never got jaded about Christmas," I say.

"Honey, if we ever felt that way," she says, "we'd sell the farm and do something else. What we do is special. And it's nice to know Caleb appreciates that."

There's a soft knock at the door. My heart pounds as Mom helps me pull the sweater over my head without messing up my hair. Before I can give her one last hug, she walks to her room and closes the door.

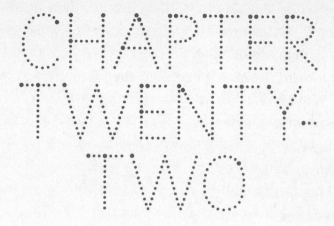

CHAPTER TWENTY-TWO

I open the door expecting to be overwhelmed at the sight of my handsome Christmas Eve date. Instead, Caleb wears a too-tight sweater of Rudolph's huge face, pulled over a purple button-down and khakis. I cover my mouth and shake my head.

He opens his arms. "Well?"

"Tell me you didn't borrow that from Heather's mom," I say.

"I did!" he says. "I really did. It was one of the few that she had with sleeves on it."

"Okay, while I love your spirit, I will not be able to focus on the service if you're wearing that."

Arms held wide, he looks down at his sweater.

"You apparently have no idea why Heather's mom owns that," I say.

He sighs and then reluctantly tugs the sweater over his chest, but it gets stuck at his ears and I have to yank it the rest of the way off. Now he is dressed like my handsome date.

It's a crisp winter evening. Many of the houses along the way kept their Christmas lights on late. Some look like their roofs are ringed in glowing icicles. Some have white-lit reindeer grazing on their lawns. My favorites are the homes that glimmer with many colors.

"You look beautiful," Caleb says. He lifts my hand as we walk and touches his lips to each finger.

"Thank you," I say. "So do you."

"See? You're getting better at taking compliments," he says.

I look over at him and smile. Blue and white lights from the nearest house reflect off his cheeks.

"Tell me about tonight," I say. "I'm guessing it'll be packed."

"They do two services on Christmas Eve," he says. "The earlier one is for families, with a pageant and a million four-year-olds dressed like angels. It's chaotic and loud and pretty perfect. The midnight mass, the one we're going to, is more solemn. It's kind of like Linus's big speech in *A Charlie Brown Christmas*."

"I love Linus," I say.

"That's good," Caleb says, "because otherwise tonight would stop right here."

We walk the rest of the way, up the gradually rising roads, hand in hand in silence. When we reach the church, the parking lot is full. Many cars are parked at the curb and even more people walk in from nearby streets.

At the church's glass doors, Caleb stops me before we enter. He looks me in the eyes. "I wish you weren't leaving," he says.

I squeeze his hand, but I don't know what to say.

He opens a door and lets me walk in first. The only light comes from candles flickering atop tall wooden rods mounted to the sides of each pew. Thick wooden beams along the walls on either side rise up, past tall windows of red, yellow, and blue stained glass. The beams touch at the center of the peaked ceiling, giving the effect of a large ship tipped upside down. At the front of the church, the edge of the stage is lined with red poinsettias. Stepped risers are already filled with a choir in white robes. Above them, an enormous wreath hangs in front of a set of brass organ pipes.

Most of the pews are packed shoulder to shoulder. We slip into a pew near the back and an elderly woman approaches us from the aisle. She hands us each an unlit white candle and a white cardboard circle about the size of my palm. In the middle of the circle is a small hole, and I watch Caleb push the top of his candle through the hole. He slides the cardboard a little more than halfway down the candle.

"These are for later," he says. "The cardboard catches the drips."

I poke my candle into the circle and then set it in my lap. "Are your mom and sister coming?"

He nods toward the choir. Abby and their mom are both

on the center riser, smiling and watching us. His mom looks so happy to be standing next to Abby. Caleb and I wave at the same time. Abby begins to wave, but her mom pulls her hand down as the choir director now stands before them.

"Abby's always been a natural singer," Caleb whispers. "She's only practiced with them twice but Mom says she blends right in."

The opening carol is "Hark! The Herald Angels Sing."

After they sing a few more songs, the pastor delivers a sincere and thoughtful talk about the story of Christmas and what the night means to him. The beauty of his words and the gratitude in how he presents them touches me. I hold on to Caleb's arm, and he looks at me with so much kindness.

The choir begins singing "We Three Kings." Caleb leans over and whispers, "Come outside with me." He takes the candle from my lap and I follow him out of the sanctuary. The glass doors close behind us and we're back in the cool air.

"What are we doing?" I ask.

He leans forward and kisses me softly. I reach up and touch his cold cheeks, which make his lips feel even warmer. I wonder if every kiss with Caleb will feel this new and magical.

He turns his head to the side, listening. "It's starting."

We walk around to the side of the church. The walls and the steeple loom over us. The narrow windows above are dark, but I know they're made of stained glass.

"What's starting?" I ask.

"It's dark in there because the ushers went around and snuffed out the candles," he says. "But listen."

He closes his eyes. I close mine, too. It's soft at first, but I hear it. It's not just the choir singing, it's the whole congregation.

"Silent night . . . Holy night."

"Right now there are two people at the front of the church holding lit candles. Only two. Everyone else has the same ones as us." He hands me my candle. I hold it near the bottom, and the cardboard circle rests atop my closed fingers. "The two people with the flames, they step into the center aisle; one heads to the pew on the left, and the other goes to the right."

"Holy infant, so tender and mild."

Caleb pulls a small booklet of matches from his front pocket, tears out a match, folds back the cover, and strikes it. He lights the wick of his candle and then shakes out the match. "The people in the first two pews, whoever is closest to the aisle, they tilt their candles to the ones with fire. Then they use that flame to light the candle of the person beside them."

"Glories stream from heaven afar."

Caleb moves his candle toward mine and I tilt mine sideways, holding the wick to his flame until it begins to burn.

"This goes on, candle by candle. It moves back row by row. The light spreads from one person to the next . . . slowly . . . creating this anticipation. You're waiting for that light to reach you."

I look at the small flame on my candle burning.

"With the dawn of redeeming grace."

"One by one, the light is passed and the entire room becomes filled with the glow."

"Jesus, Lord, at Thy birth."

His voice is soft. "Look up."

I look to the stained glass windows. There's now a warm glow coming from inside. The glass shimmers in reds, yellows, and blues. The song continues and I hold my breath.

"Silent night . . . Holy night."

The lyrics are sung all the way through one more time. Eventually, inside the church and out here, there is total silence.

Caleb leans forward. With a soft breath, he blows out his candle. Then I blow out mine.

"I'm glad we came out here," I say.

He pulls me close and kisses me softly, holding his lips against mine for several seconds.

Still holding each other, I lean back and ask, "But why didn't you want me to see this from inside?"

"For the past few years, I never felt as calm as the moment my candle got lit on Christmas Eve. For just an instant, everything was okay." He pulls himself close, his chin on my shoulder, and whispers into my ear, "This year, I wanted to spend that moment only with you."

"Thank you," I whisper. "It was perfect."

CHAPTER TWENTY-THREE

The church doors open and the Christmas Eve service is over. It's after midnight and the people leaving must be tired, but each face looks filled with a peaceful happiness—with joy. Most of them don't say anything as they walk to their cars, but there are several tender wishes of "Merry Christmas."

It is Christmas.

My last day.

I see Jeremiah hold the door open for a few people, and then he walks over to us. "I saw you duck out," he says. "You missed the best part."

I look at Caleb. "Did we miss the best part?"

"I don't think we did," he says.

I smile at Jeremiah. "No, we didn't miss it."

Jeremiah shakes Caleb's hand and then pulls him into a hug. "Merry Christmas, friend."

Caleb says nothing; he just hugs and closes his eyes.

Jeremiah pats him on the back, and then he wraps me in a hug. "Merry Christmas, Sierra."

"Merry Christmas, Jeremiah."

"I'll see you in the morning," he tells me, and then he walks back into the church.

"We should start heading back," Caleb says.

There's no way to describe how much tonight has meant to me. In this moment, I want to tell Caleb that I love him. This would be the time, right here, because this is when I first know it's true.

I can't say it, though. It's not fair for him to hear those words and then have me leave so soon after. Saying it would also sear them onto my heart. I would think of those words the entire ride home.

"I wish I could stop time," I say instead. It's the most I can give either of us.

"Me too." He takes my hand. "What's next for us? Do we know?"

I wish he could give me the answer to that question. It feels too insignificant to say we'll keep in touch. I know we will, but what more?

I shake my head. "I don't know."

When we get back to the tree lot, Caleb kisses me and then takes a step back. It feels right for him to start pulling away. There is no Christmas miracle that can keep me here or guarantee us more than we have now.

"Good night, Sierra."

I can't say that back. "We'll see each other tomorrow," I say.

As he walks to his truck, his head is bowed, and I see him look at the picture of us on his keychain. After he opens his door, he turns to me one more time.

"Good night," he says.

"I'll see you in the morning."

I wake with a mix of clashing emotions. I eat a small breakfast of oatmeal with brown sugar before heading over to Heather's house. When I get there, she's sitting on her front stoop waiting for me.

Without getting up, she says, "You're leaving me again."

"I know."

"And this time, we don't know when you're coming back," she says. She finally stands and holds me in a long hug.

Caleb's truck pulls into the driveway with Devon riding shotgun. The two of them get out, each holding a few small wrapped gifts. Whatever sadness Caleb carried as he drove away last night seems to have disappeared.

"Merry Christmas!" he says.

"Merry Christmas," Heather and I say.

Both guys give us each pecks on the cheek, and then Heather ushers us into her kitchen, where coffeecake and hot chocolate are waiting. Caleb declines the coffeecake because he had an omelet and French toast with his mom and Abby.

"It's a tradition," he says, but he does drop a peppermint stick into his hot chocolate.

"Have you jumped on the trampoline today?" I ask.

"Abby and I had a backflip contest first thing." He holds his stomach. "Which wasn't the smartest thing to do after breakfast, but it was fun."

Heather and Devon sit back in their chairs, watching us talk. It could be one of our last conversations and they seem in no rush to interrupt.

"Did you tell your mom you'd already found it?" I ask.

He sips his hot chocolate and smiles. "She threatened to give me all gift cards next year."

"Well, she found the perfect gift this year," I say. I lean over and give him a kiss.

"And on that note," Heather says, "it's time for *our* gifts."

I almost can't watch as Devon begins unwrapping his floppy-looking present. He draws out the uneven and still-too-short red-and-green scarf. He tips his head, turning it over and over. Then he smiles, possibly the biggest, most genuine smile I've seen on his lips. "Baby, you made this?"

Heather smiles back and shrugs.

"I love it!" He drapes the scarf around his neck and it barely hangs past his collarbone. "No one's ever knit me a scarf before. I can't believe how much time you must've spent on this."

Heather is beaming and looks my way. I give her a nod

and she scoots herself into Devon's lap, hugging him. "I have been such a bad girlfriend," she says. "I'm sorry. I promise to be better."

Devon pulls back, confused. He touches the scarf. "I said I liked it."

Heather moves back to her seat and then gives him an envelope with the comedy show tickets inside. He seems pleased by that, too, but not as much as by the scarf he continues to wear proudly.

Heather hands an envelope across the table to me. "It's not for right now," she says, "but I hope you'll look forward to it."

I open a printout that has been folded into thirds. It takes me a few seconds to decipher that it's a receipt for a train ticket from here to Oregon. Over spring break! "You're coming up to see me?"

Heather does a little shimmy dance in her seat.

I walk around to Heather and hug her so tight. I want to see Caleb's reaction to her coming up to see me but I know I would overanalyze any look on his face. So I give Heather a kiss on the cheek and hug her again.

Devon places a small cylindrical gift in front of Caleb and then one in front of Heather. "I know we already had our perfect day, but I got the same thing for you and Caleb."

Caleb weighs it in his hand.

Devon looks at me. "It actually has to do with you, Sierra."

Caleb and Heather unwrap their gifts at the same time: *A Very Special Christmas* scented candles.

Caleb inhales deeply and then looks at me. "Yep. This'll drive me crazy."

I grab a candy cane, put it in my cup, and stir. I feel so overwhelmed at this moment. The morning is moving too fast, but it's my turn to give presents now. I push one of the small wrapped boxes across the table to Heather.

"Good things come in small packages," she says. She rips into the wrapping paper and then opens a hinged black velvet box. She holds up a silver bracelet that I bought downtown, where I also had it engraved with latitude and longitude: *45.5° N, 123.1°W.*

"Those are the coordinates to our farm," I say. "Now you can always find your way to me."

She looks at me and whispers, "Always."

I hand Caleb his gift. He's meticulous about removing the wrapping, taking off one piece of tape at a time. Heather's shoe touches mine beneath the table, but I can't stop watching Caleb.

"Before you look inside," I tell him, "don't expect it to have cost anything."

He dimple-smiles and takes out the glittery red box.

"But it took a lot of care," I say, "and a lot of tears, and a lot of memories that I will never let go of."

He looks down at the box, with the top still on. When his dimple fades, I think he knows what's inside. If he does, he knows how much it means that I'm giving it to him. He carefully lifts off the top. The painted-on Christmas tree is faceup.

I look over at Heather. Her hands are clasped and pressed against her lips.

Devon looks at me. "I don't get it."

Heather hits him on the shoulder. "Later."

Caleb looks stunned, his eyes staying on the gift. "I thought this was in Oregon."

"It was," I say. "But it needs to be here." The gift that arrived with it, tickets to a dance that I don't know if I'll attend, is still in the trailer hidden behind our picture with Santa.

He lifts the tree cutting from the box, his fingertips holding the bark ring. "This is irreplaceable," he says.

"It is," I say, "and it's yours."

He hands me an unwrapped sparkly green box held together with red ribbon. I slide off the ribbon and then pull off the top. Resting on a thin layer of cotton is another tree cutting, from a tree about the same size as the one I gave him. There's a Christmas tree painted in the middle with an angel perched on top. I look at him, confused.

"I went back to your tree on Cardinals Peak," he says. "The one that was cut. Part of it needs to return home with you."

Now Heather and I both put a hand over our mouths. Devon drums his fingers on the table.

"A few weeks ago, I bought you something else," Caleb says. He pulls out a nearly see-through gold cloth bag. "Note, this bag is diaphanous."

I laugh. "It is very diaphanous," I say. Through the delicate fabric I can see a golden necklace. I loosen the drawstrings that hold the bag shut and shake out a necklace with a small pendant of a duck in flight.

His voice is soft. "Something else we wait on to come south every winter."

I meet his stare, and it feels like Heather and Devon aren't even in the room with us.

Heather takes the cue. "Babe, come help me find some Christmas music."

Without breaking eye contact, I slip into Caleb's arms and kiss him. Then I bring my head to his shoulder, wishing I never had to leave this spot.

"Thank you for the present," he says.

"Thank you for mine."

A slow Christmas instrumental begins in the next room. Caleb and I don't move until after the third song begins.

"Can I drive you back?" he asks.

I sit up and pull my hair away from my neck. "Will you put the necklace on me first?"

Caleb hangs the pendant below my collarbone and then secures the clasp behind my neck. I try to memorize every brush of his fingertips against my skin. We grab our coats and then say goodbye to Heather and Devon, who lean against each other on the couch.

The short drive back feels lonely even though Caleb is right beside me. It feels like we're in the process of returning to our own worlds. I touch my necklace several times and see him glance at me each time I do it.

I step out of the truck. When my feet touch the dirt I feel glued to the earth. "I don't want this to be it," I say.

"Does it have to be?" he asks.

"You've got dinner with your mom and Abby, and we'll be working all night to take this place down," I say. "Mom and I leave in the morning."

"Do me a favor," he says.

I wait.

"Believe in us."

I nod and bite my lip. I step back and close my door, offering a small wave. He drives away and I say a prayer.

Please. Don't let this be the last time I see Caleb.

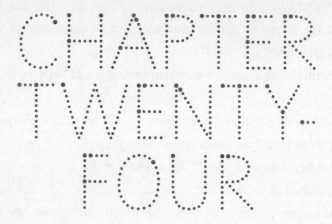

CHAPTER TWENTY-FOUR

Several of the ballplayers, plus Luis and Jeremiah, work on lowering the Bigtop. Others take down the snowflake lights and wrap up the cords. I help people who come to take our remaining trees. For a few dollars each, they can let them dry out for bonfires. Employees from City Parks bring their trucks and we load them up with trees to submerge in nearby lakes as reefs.

I notice my fingers touching my necklace several times throughout the morning and afternoon. For dinner my parents and I have Chinese takeout in the trailer, and then a bunch of workers return after their family dinners. Like every year, we build a bonfire in the almost empty lot. We sit on wooden benches and folding chairs around the fire and roast marshmallows. Luis passes around a box of graham crackers and hands out chocolate for s'mores. Heather and Devon came by and are already bickering over what to do for New Year's. He wants to watch football but she wants to start the year with a hike.

Jeremiah sits next to me. "You look too sad for Christmas, Sierra."

"I've always hated the letdown after Christmas morning," I say. "This year has been especially rough."

"All because of Caleb?" he asks.

"Caleb. This town. Because of everything." I look at the people sitting around the fire. "I kind of fell in love with my time here in a way I never have before."

"How are you with advice?" he asks.

I look to him. "Depends on the advice."

"As someone who's lost a whole bunch of time with Caleb, and who's going to have to fight for more, I can only say do everything you can to hang on to him. You're really good for him," he says, "and he seems good for you."

I nod, swallowing past the lump in my throat. "He is good for me," I say, "I know that. But logically, how can—"

"Forget logic," he says. "Logic doesn't know what you want."

"I know. And it's not just a want," I say. I look into the fire. "It's more than that."

"Then you're lucky," he says, "because someone we both care a lot about more than wants the same thing."

He taps me on the shoulder. When I look at him, he points a finger toward the dark silhouette of Cardinals Peak. Near the top are hundreds of colored sparkling lights.

I put my hand against my heart. "Are those my trees?"

"They just turned on," he says.

My phone buzzes in my pocket. I look at Jeremiah and he shrugs. I pull out my phone and see a text from Caleb: **Your tree family and I miss you already.**

I jump to my feet. "He's up there! I have to see him."

Mom and Dad sit at the opposite side of the bonfire, a single long scarf keeping both of them warm.

"Is it okay if . . . ? I need to . . ." I gesture toward Cardinals Peak. "He . . ."

They both smile at me and Mom says, "We have an early morning tomorrow. Don't be out too late."

"Make good choices," Dad says, and Mom and I laugh.

I glance at Heather and Devon. He's got an arm around her and she's tucked herself against him. Before I leave, I give my two friends a double-hug.

Heather makes sure my parents can't hear, and then whispers in my ear, "Keep each other warm."

I look to Jeremiah. "Can you drive me?"

"My pleasure," he says.

"Okay," I tell him, "but I need to grab something first."

It feels like it takes longer than ever to drive from the lot to the gate at the base of Cardinals Peak.

When Jeremiah pulls onto the dirt and grass, he says, "You're on your own, lot girl. I will not be a third wheel for this." We both look up at the hill, to the distant lights on my trees. He reaches to open the glove box and then hands me a small flashlight.

I lean over and give him a hug. "Thank you."

The flashlight turns right on. I hop out of his car and shut the door, and then he backs away. When the taillights fade, it's just me, this tiny light, and a looming hill. The hill is dark except for one patch of colorful lights on my trees, with a very special person up there waiting for me.

I reach the last several yards before the final turn in the road, feeling like I must have flown up the hill. Caleb's truck is parked ahead of me. The passenger window is open and a long power cord drapes down the door and into the brush where Caleb stands, facing away from me and toward the town. The Christmas lights on my trees are bright enough that I can turn off the flashlight and see my way safely to him. He looks down at his phone, probably waiting for a response.

"You are amazing," I say.

He turns around, his smile bright.

"I thought you were with your family," I say, stepping into the brush.

"I was. But apparently I looked distracted," he says. "Abby told me to stop moping around and go see you. I figured this was a better way to have you come see me."

"You definitely drew me in."

He takes a step toward me, the lights dancing across his face. We both reach for each other's hands and pull each other closer. We kiss, and this one kiss melts away everything I've been unsure of. I want this.

I want us.

I whisper into his ear, "I have something for you, too." I reach into my back pocket and remove a folded envelope.

When he takes it, I turn on the flashlight and shine it at his hands. His fingers shake, either from cold or anticipation. It makes me happy that I may not be the only one on this hill who's nervous. He pulls out the tickets to the winter formal, with the couple dancing together in the snow globe. He looks at me, and I know we have matching grins.

"Caleb, will you be my date to the winter dance?" I ask. "I won't go with anyone else."

"I would be your date to anything," he says.

We hold on to each other in a tight, warm hug.

"You'll really go?" I ask.

He pulls his head back and smiles at me. "What else am I going to save my tips for?"

I look into his eyes, and it comes out as a statement. "You know I love you."

He leans forward and whispers into my ear. "You know I love you, too."

He kisses me on the neck and then I wait while he walks to his truck. He leans into the open window, turns the key, and the stereo comes on. "It's the Most Wonderful Time of the Year" plays into the cold night air around us. I stifle a laugh, and Caleb smiles.

"Go ahead," he says, "tell me I'm cheesy."

"Did you forget?" I say. "My family survives on this stuff."

In the town below, I can see the flickering bonfire where Mom, Dad, and some of my best friends in the world are keeping warm. Maybe they're looking up here right now. If they are, I hope they're smiling because I'm smiling right back.

"Dance with me?" Caleb asks.

I hold out my hand. "We may as well practice."

He takes my hand, spins me around once, and then we move together. The Christmas lights sparkle on my trees, which dance along with us in the gentle wind.

THE END

The Nice List

Ben Schrank, publisher, and Laura Rennert, literary agent
for being with me wholly since Book 1,
and for being my insecure-author therapists as needed

Jessica Almon, editor
when I questioned, you believed;
when I was done, you rightly pushed for more
"It reminds me of a Taylor Swift song!"

Mom, Dad, and Nate
(and my cousins, aunts, uncles,
grandparents, neighbors, friends . . .)
for my childhood of holiday magic

Luke Gies, Amy Kearley, Tom Morris, Aaron Porter,
Matt Warren, Mary Weber, DonnaJo Woollen
my guiding angels

Hopper Bros.—Woodburn, OR
Heritage Plantations—Forest Grove, OR
Halloway's Christmas Trees—Nipomo, CA
Thorntons' Treeland—Vancouver, WA
for tours of your Christmas tree farms and
answers to professional, personal, and silly (but legit!) questions

Ten years ago, one book sparked a conversation
that's been changing readers' lives ever since.

Join the millions who are talking about
Thirteen Reasons Why
with this special anniversary edition.